THE IMITATOR: /
BY
Percival Pollarc

THE IMITATOR: A NOVEL

Published by Chasma Press

New York City, NY

First published circa 1911

Copyright © Chasma Press, 2015

All rights reserved

ABOUT CHASMA PRESS

No genre has ever unlocked the possibilities and potential of mankind like science fiction. Sci-fi writers like H.G. Wells and Jules Verne have been conjuring up vivid depictions of the future for centuries, and **Chasma Press** brings all these worlds to life to readers who continue to read the classics and forge visions of new ones.

CHAPTER I.

The thing is already on the wane," said young Orson Vane, making a wry face over the entree,
l sniffing at his glass, "and, if you ask me, I think the general digestion of society will be the
ter for it."

Yes, there is nothing, after all, so tedious as the sham variety of a table d'hote. Though it
tainly wasn't the fare one came to this hole for."

uke Moncreith turned his eyes, as he said that, over the place they sat in, smiling at it with
newhat melancholy contempt. Its sanded floor, its boisterously exposed wine-barrels, the
aningless vivacity of its Hungarian orchestra, evidently stirred him no more.

No; that was the last detail. It was the notion of dining below stairs, as the servants do. It had,
a time, the charm of an imitation. Nothing is so delightful as to imitate others; yet to be
staken for them is always dreadful. Of course, nobody would mistake us here for servants."

The company, motley as it was, could not logically have come under any such suspicion.
ough it was dining in a cellar, on a sanded floor, amid externals that were illegitimate
springs of a Studenten Kneipe and a crew of Christy minstrels, it still had, in the main, the air
being recruited from the smart world. At every other table there were people whom not to
ow was to argue oneself unknown. These persons obviously treated the place, and their being
re, as an elaborate effort at gaiety; the others, the people who were plainly there for the first
ie, took it with the bewildered manner of those whom each new experience leaves mentally
iausted. The touch of rusticity, here and there, did not suffice to spoil the sartorial sparkle of
: smart majority. The champagne that the sophisticated were wise enough to oppose to the
igyar vintages sparkled into veins that ran beautifully blue under skin that held curves the
ist aristocratic, tints the most shell-like. Tinkling laughter, vocative of insincerity, rang
ween the restless passion of the violins.

When it is not below stairs," continued Vane, "it is up on the roof. One might think we were a
iety without houses of our own. It is, I suppose, the human craving for opposites. When we
ve stored our sideboards with the finest glass you can get in Vienna or Carlsbad, we turn our
:ks on it and go to drinking from pewter in a cellar. We pay abominable wages to have
vants who shall be noiseless, and then go to places where the service is as guttural as a
lderness of monkeys. Fortunately, these fancies do not last. Presently, I dare say, it will be the
hion to dine at home. That will make us feel quite like the original Puritans." He laughed, and
ik his glass of wine at a gulp. "The fact of the matter is that variety has become the vice of life.
: have not, as a society, any inner steadfastness of soul; we depend upon externals, and the
:ernals pall with fearful speed. Think of seeing in the mirror the face of the same butler for
ire than thirty days!" He shuddered and shook his head.

We are a restless lot," sighed the other, "but why discompose yourself about it? Thank your
rs you have nothing more important to worry over!"

My dear Luke, there is nothing more important than the attitude of society at large. It is the
ly thing one should allow oneself to discuss. To consider one's individual life is to be guilty of

as bad form as to wear anything that is conspicuous. Society admires us chiefly only as we sink ourselves in it. If we let the note of personality rise, our social position is sure to suffer. Imitation is the keynote of smartness. The rank and file imitate the leaders consciously, and the leaders unconsciously imitate the average. We frequent cellars, and roofs, and such places, because in doing so we imagine we are imitating the days of the Hanging Gardens and the Catacombs. We abhor the bohemian taint, but we are willing to give a champagne and chicken imitation of it. We do not really care for music and musicians, but we give excellent imitations of doing so. At present we are giving the most lifelike imitation of being passionately fond of outdoor life; I suppose England feels flattered. I am afraid I have forgotten whose the first fashionable divorce in our world was; it is far easier to remember the names of the people who have never been divorced; at any rate those pioneers ought to feel proud of the hugeness of their following. We have adopted a vulgarity from Chicago and made it a fashionable institution; divorce used to be a shuttlecock for the comic papers, and now it makes the bulk of the social register."

Moncreith tapped his friend on the arm. "Drop it, Orson, drop it!" he said. "I know this is a beastly bad dinner, but you shouldn't let it make you maudlin. You know you don't really believe half you're saying. Drop it, I say. These infernal poses make me ill." He attacked the morsel of game on his plate with a zest that was beautiful to behold. "If you go on in that biliously philosophic strain of yours, I shall crunch this bird until I hear nothing but the grinding of bones. It is really not a bad bit of quail. It is so small, and the casserole so large, that you need an English setter to mark it, but once you've got it,"—he wiped his lips with a flip of his napkin, "it's really worth the search. Try it, and cheer up. The woman in rose, over there, under the pseudo-palm, looks at you every time she sips her champagne; I have no doubt she is calculating how untrue you could be to her. I suppose your gloom strikes her as poetic; it strikes me as very absurd. You really haven't a care in the world, and you sit here spouting insincerity at a wasteful rate. If there's anything really and truly the matter—tell me!"

Orson Vane dropped, as if it had been a mask, the ironical smile his lips had worn. "You want sincerity," he said, "well, then I shall be sincere. Sincerity makes wrinkles, but it is the privilege of our friends to make us old before our time. Sincerely, then, Luke, I am very, very tired."

"A fashionable imitation," mocked Moncreith.

"No; a personal aversion, to myself, to the world I live in. I wish the dear old governor hadn't been such a fine fellow; if he had been of the newer generation of fathers I suppose I wouldn't have had an ideal to bless myself with."

Moncreith interrupted.

"Good Lord, Luke, did you say ideals? I swear I never knew it was as bad as that." He beckoned to the waiter and ordered a Dominican. "It is so ideal a liquor that when you have tasted it you crave only for brutalities. Poor Orson! Ideals!" He sighed elaborately.

"If you imitate my manner of a while ago, I shall not say what I was going to say. If I am to be sincere, so must you." He took the scarlet drink the man set before him, and let it gurgle gently down his throat. "It smacks of sin and I scent lies in it. I wish I had not taken it. It is hard to be sincere after a drink that stirs the imagination. But I shall try. And you are not to interrupt any

re than you can help. If we both shed the outer skin we wear for society, I believe we are
ther of us such bad sorts. That is just what I am getting at: I am not quite bad enough to be
nd to my own futility. Here I am, Luke, young, decently looking, with money, position, and
lily health, and yet I am cursed with thought of my own futility. When people have said who I
, they have said it all; I have done nothing: I merely am. I know others would sell their souls
be what I am; but it does not content me. I have spent years considering my way. The arts
ve called to me, but they have not held me. All arts are imitative, except music, and music is
t human enough for me; no people are so unhuman as musical people, and no art is so entirely
reation of a self-centred inventor. There can be no such thing as realism in music; the voices
Nature can never be equalled on any humanly devised instruments or notes. Painting and
llpture are mere imitations of what nature does far better. When you see a beautiful woman as
d made her you do not care whether the Greeks colored their statues or not. Any average
lset stamps the painted imitation as absurd. These arts, in fact, can never be really great, since
y are man's feeble efforts to copy God's finest creations; between them and the ideal there
lst always be the same distance as between man and his Creator. Then there is the art of
rature. It has the widest scope of them all. Whether it is imitative or creative depends on the
lperament of the individual; some men set down what they see and hear, others invent a world
their own and busy themselves with it. I believe it is the most human of the arts. Its devotees
t infrequently set themselves the task of discovering just how their fellows think and live; they
to attune their souls to other souls; they strive for an understanding of the larger humanity.
ey—"
Moncreith interrupted with a gesture.
Orson, you're not going to turn novelist? Don't tell me that! Your enthusiasms fill me with
lancholy forebodings."
Not at all. But, as you know, I've seen much of this sort of thing lately. In the first place I had
own temperamental leanings; in the next place, you'll remember, we've had a season or two
ely when clever people have been the rage. To invite painters and singers and writers to one's
use has been the smart thing to do. We have had the spectacle of a society, that goes through a
pant imitation of living, engaged in being polite to people who imitate at second hand, in
1g, and color, and story. Some smart people have even taken to those arts, thus imitating the
fessional imitators. As far as the smart point of view goes, I couldn't do anything better than
in for the studio, or novelistic business. The dull people whom smartness has rubbed to a thin
lish would conspire in calling me clever. Is there anything more dreadful than being called
ver?"
Nothing. It is the most damning adjective in the language. Whenever I hear that a person is
ver I am sure he will never amount to much. There is only one word that approaches it in
idly significance. That is 'rising.' I have known men whom the puffs have referred to as 'a
ng man' for twenty years. Can you imagine anything more dismal than being called constantly
the same epithet? The very amiability in the general opinion, permitting 'clever' and 'rising' to
lain unalterable, shows that the wearer of these terms is hopeless; a strong man would have

made enemies. I am glad you are wise enough to resist the temptation of the Muses. Society's blessing would never console you for anything short of a triumph. The triumphs are fearfully few; the clever people—well, this cellar's full of them. There's Abbott Moore, for instance."

"You're right; there he is. He's a case in point. One of the best cases; a man who has really, in the worldly sense, succeeded tremendously. His system of give and take is one of the most lovely schemes imaginable; we all know that. When a mining millionaire with marriageable daughters comes to town his first hostage to the smart set is to order a palace near Central Park and to give Abbott Moore the contract for the decorations. In return Abbott Moore asks the millionaire's womenfolk to one of his studio carnivals. That section of the smart set which keeps itself constantly poised on the border between smart and tart is awfully keen on Abbott Moore's studio affairs. It has never forgotten the famous episode when he served a tart within a tart, and it is still expecting him to outdo that feat. To be seen at one of these affairs, especially if you have millions, is to have got in the point of the wedge. I call it a fair exchange; the millionaire gets his foot just inside the magic portal; Moore gets a slice of the millions. All the world counts Moore a success from every point of view, the smart, the professional, the financial. Yet that isn't my notion of a full life. It's only a replica of the very thing I'm tired of, my own life."

"Your life, my dear fellow, is generally considered a most enviable article."

"Of course. I suppose it does have a glamour for the unobserving. Yet, at the best, what am I?"

Moncreith laughed. "Another Dominican!" he said to the waiter. "The liqueur," he said, "may enable me to rise to my subject." He smiled at Vane over the glass, when it was brought to him, drained it under closed eyes, and then settled himself well back into his chair.

CHAPTER II.

I will tell you what you are," began Moncreith, "to I the eye of the average beholder. Here, in
 most splendid town of the western world, at the turning of two centuries, you are possessed
youth, health and wealth. That really tells the tale. Never in the history of the world have
uth and health and wealth meant so much as they do now. These three open the gates to all the
thly paradise. Your forbears did their duty by you so admirably that you wear a distinguished
me without any sacrifice to poverty. You are good to look at. You are a young man of fashion.
you chose you could lead the mode; you have the instincts of a beau, though neither the severe
pression of Brummell nor the obtrusive splendor of D'Aurevilly would suit you. Our age
ms to have come to too high an average in man's apparel to permit of any single dictator; to
singled out is to be lowered. Yet there can be no denying that you have often, unwittingly, set
 fashion in waistcoats and cravats. That aping has not hurt you, because the others never gave
ir raiment the fine note of personal distinction that you wear. You are a favorite in the clubs;
ple never go out when you come in; you listen to the most stupid talk with the most graceful
imaginable; that is one of the sure roads to popularity in clubdom. When it is the fashion to be
istic, you can be so as easily as the others; when sport is the watchword your fine physique
bids you no achievement. You play tennis and golf and polo quite well enough to make
men split their gloves in applause, and not too well to make men sneer at you for a 'pro.'
en you are riding to hounds in Virginia you are never far from the kill, and there is no
omobilist whom the Newport villagers are happier to fine for fast driving. You are equally at
me in a cotillon and on the deck of a racing yacht. You could marry whenever you liked. Your
aracter is unspotted either by the excessive vice that shocks the mob, or the excessive virtue
t tires the smart. You have means, manners and manner. Finally, you have the two cardinal
alities of smartness, levity and tolerance." He paused, and gave a smile of satisfaction. "There,
you like the portrait?"

It is abominable," said Vane, "it is what I see in my most awful dreams. And the horror of it is
t it is so frightfully true. I am merely one of the figures in the elaborate masquerade we call
iety. I make no progress in life; I learn nothing except new fashions and foibles. I am weary
the masquerade and the masks. Life in the smart world is a game with masks; one shuffles
m as one does cards. As for me, I want to throw the whole pack into the fire. Everyone wears
se masks; nobody ever penetrates to the real soul behind the make-up."

It is a game you play perfectly. One should hesitate long about giving up anything that one
 brought to perfection. These others dabble and squabble in what you call the secondary
itations of life; you, at any rate, are giving your imitation at first hand."

Yes, but it no longer satisfies me. Listen, Luke. You must promise not to laugh and not to
wn. It will seem absurd to you; yet I am terribly in earnest about it. When first I came out of
lege I went in for science. When I gave it up, it was because I found it was leading me away
m the human interest. There is the butterfly I want to chase; the human interest. I attempted all
 arts; not one of them took me far on my way. My failure, Luke, is an ironic sentence upon the

vaunted knowledge of the world."

"Your failure? My dear Orson; come to the point. What do you mean by the human interest?"

"I mean that neither scientist nor scholar has yet shown the way to one man's understanding of another's soul. The surgeon can take a body and dissect its every fraction, arguing and proving each function of it. The painter tries, with feeble success, to reach what he calls the spirit of his subject. So does the author. He tries to put himself into the place of each of his characters; he aims, always, for the nearest possible approach to the lifelike. And, above all the others, there is the actor. In this, as in its other qualities, the art of acting is the crudest, the most obvious of them all; yet, in certain moments, it comes nearest to the ideal. The actor in his mere self is—well, we all know the story of the famous player being met by this greeting: 'And what art thou to-night?' But he goes behind a door and he can come forth in a series of selves. A trick or so with paint; a change of wig; a twist of the face-muscles, and we have the same man appearing as Napoleon, as Richelieu, as Falstaff. The thing is external, of course. Whether there shall be anything more than the mere bodily mask depends upon the actor's intelligence and his imagination. The supreme artist so succeeds, by virtue of much study, much skill in imitating what he has conceived to be the soul of his subject, in almost giving us a lifelike portrait. And yet, and yet—it is not the real thing; the real soul of his subject is as much a mystery to that actor as it is to you or me. That is what I mean when I say that science fails us at the most important point of all; the soul of my neighbor is as profound a mystery to me as the soul of a man that lived a thousand years ago. I can know your face, Luke, your clothes, your voice, the outward mask you wear; but—can I reach the secrets of your soul? No. And if we cannot know how others feel and think, how can we say we know the world? Bah! The world is a realm of shadows in which all walk blindly. We touch hands every day, but our souls are hidden in a veil that has not been passed since God made the universe."

"You cry for the moon," said Moncreith. "You long for the unspeakable. Is it not terrible enough to know your neighbor's face, his voice, his coat, without burdening yourself with knowledge of his inner self? It is merely an egoistic curiosity, my dear Orson; you cannot prove that the human interest, as you term it, would benefit by the extension in wisdom you want."

"Oh, you are wrong, you are wrong. The whole world of science undergoes revolution, once you gain the point I speak of. Doctors will have the mind as well as the body to diagnose; lovers will read each others hearts as well as their voices; lies will become impossible, or, at least, futile; oh—it would be a better world altogether. At any rate, until this avenue of knowledge is opened to me, I shall call all the rest a failure. I imitate; you imitate; we imitate; that is the conjugation of life. When I think of the hopelessness of the thing,—do you wonder I grow bitter? I want communion with real beings, and I meet only masks. I tell you, Luke, it is abominable, this wall that stands between each individual and the rest of the world. How can I love my neighbor if I do not understand him? How can I understand him if I cannot think his thoughts, dream his dreams, spell out his soul's secrets?"

Moncreith smiled at his friend, and let his eyes wander a trifle ironically about his figure. "One would not think, to look at you, that you were possessed of a mania, an itch! If you take my

vice you will content yourself with living life as you find it. It is really a very decent world. It
s good meat and drink in it, and some sweet women, and a strong man or two. Most of us are
ite ignorant of the fact that we are merely engaged in incomplete imitations of life, or that
re is a Chinese wall between us and the others; the chances are we are all the happier for our
ocence. Consider, for instance, that rosy little face behind us—you can see it perfectly in that
rror—can you deny that it looks all happiness and innocence?"

/ane looked, and presently sighed a little. The face of the girl, as he found it in the glass, was
: color of roses lying on a pool of clear water. It was one of those faces that one scarce knows
ether to think finer in profile or in full view; the features were small, the hair glistened with a
t of that burnish the moon sometimes wears on summer nights, and the figure was a mere fillip
the imagination. A cluster of lilies of the valley lay upon her hair; they seemed like countless
le cups pouring frost upon a copper glow. All about her radiated an ineffable gentleness, a
derness; she made all the other folk about her seem garish and ugly and cruel. One wondered
at she did in that gallery.

To the outer eye," said Vane, as he sighed, "she is certainly a flower, a thing of daintiness and
ight. But—do you suppose I believe it, for a moment? I have no doubt she is merely one of
se creatures whom God has made for the destruction of our dreams; her mind is probably as
rupt as her body seems fair. She is perhaps—"

le stopped, for the face in the mirror had its eyes thrown suddenly in his direction. The eyes,
that reflex fashion, met, and something akin to a smile, oh, an ever so wistful, wonderful a
ile, crept upon the lips and the eyes of the girl, while to the man there came only a sudden
nce.

She is," continued Vane, in another voice altogether, and as if he were thinking of distant
airs, "very beautiful."

he girl's eyes, meanwhile, had shifted towards Moncreith. He felt the radiance of them and
ked, too, and the girl's beauty came upon him with a quick, personal force that was like pain.
ne's spoken approbation of her angered him; he hardly knew why; for the first time in his life
thought he could hate the man beside him.

he girl turned her head a little, put up her hand and so hid her face from both young men, or
re is no telling what sudden excuse the two might not have seized for open enmity. It sounds
itastic, perhaps, but there are more enmities sown in a single glance from a woman's eyes than
Aachiavelli could build up by ever so devilish devices. Neither of the two, in this case, could
ve said just what they felt, or why. Moncreith thought, vaguely enough perhaps, that it was a
for so fair a flower to waste even a look upon a fellow so shorn of faith as was Orson Vane.
for Vane—

/ane brought his hand upon the table so that the glasses rocked.

Oh," he exclaimed, "if one could only be sure! If one could see past the mask! What would I
t give to believe in beauty when I see it, to trust to appearances! Oh, for the ability to put
self in the place of another, to know life from another plane than my own, to—"

}ut here he was interrupted.

CHAPTER III

The secret you are seeking," said the man who had put his hand on Orson Vane's shoulder, "is
ne."

Vane's eyes widened slightly, roving the stranger up and down. He was a man of six feet in
ght, of striking, white-haired beauty, of the type made familiar to us by pictures of the Old
ard under Napoleon. Here was still the Imperial under the strong chin, the white mustache
er the shapely lips; the high, clear forehead; the long, thin hands, where veins showed blue,
l the nails were rosy. The head was bowed forward of the shoulders; the man, now old, had
ce been inches taller. You looked, on the spur of first noting him, for the sword and the
ulets, or, at least, for the ribbon of an order. But his clothes were quite plain, nor had his
ice any touch of the military.

I overheard a part of your conversation," the stranger went on, "not intentionally, yet
avoidably. I had either to move or to listen. And you see the place is so full that moving was
of the question. Did you mean what you were saying?"

About the—"

The Chinese wall," said the stranger.

Every word of it," said Vane.

If the chance to penetrate another's soul came to you, would you take it?"

At once."

Moncreith laughed aloud. "Where are we?" he said, "in Aladdin's cave? What rubbish!" And he
ook himself, as if to disturb a bad dream. He was on the point of reaching for his hat, when he
v the face of the girl in the mirror once more; the sight of it stayed him. He smiled to himself,
d waited for the curious conversation between Vane and the stranger to continue.

My name," the stranger was observing, taking a card from an etui, "may possibly be known to
u?"

Vane bent his head to the table, read, and looked at the white-haired man with a quick access
interest.

I am honored," he said. "My name is Orson Vane."

Oh," said the other, "I knew that. I do not study the human interest in mere theory; I delight in
tangible. That is why I presume upon you"—he waved his hand gracefully—"thus."

You must join us," said Vane; "there is plenty of room at this table."

No; I must—if your friend will pardon me—see you alone. Will you come to my place?"

He spoke as youthfully as if he were of Vane's own age.

Vane considered a second or so, and then sprang to his feet.

Yes," he said, "I will come. Good-night, Luke. Stay on; enjoy yourself. Shall I see you to-
rrow? Good-night!"

hey went out together, the young man and the one with the white hair. One glance into the
rror flashed from Orson's eyes as he turned to go; it brought him a memory of a burnished
o on a fragile, rosy, beauty. He sighed to himself, wishing he could reach the truth behind the

robe of beauty, and, with that sigh, turned with a sort of fierceness upon his companion.

"Well," said Vane, "well?"

They were passing through a most motley thoroughfare. Barrel-organs dotted the asphalt; Italian and Sicilian poverty elbowed the poverty of Russian and Polish Jews. The shops bore signs in Italian, Hebrew, French—in anything but English. The Elevated roared above the music and the chatter; the cool gloom of lower Broadway seemed far away.

"Patience," said the old man, "patience, Mr. Vane. Look about you! How much of the heart of this humanity that reeks all about us do we know? Think,—think of your Chinese wall! Oh—how strange, how very strange that I should have come upon you to-night, when, in despair of ever finding my man, I had gone for distraction to a place where, I thought, philosophy nor science were but little welcome."

"My dear Professor," urged Vane finally, when they were come to a stiller region, where many churches, some parks and ivy-sheltered houses gave an air of age and sobriety and history, "I have no more patience left. Did I not know your name for what it is I would not have followed you. Even now I hardly know whether your name and your title suffice. If it is an adventure, very well. But I have no more patience for mysteries."

"Not even when you are about to penetrate the greatest mystery of all? Oh, youth, youth! Well, we have still a little distance to go. I shall employ it to impress upon you that I, Professor Vanlief, am not over-fond of the title of Professor. It has, here in America, a taint of the charlatan. But it came to me, this title, in a place where only honors were implied. I was, indeed, a fellow student with many of whom the world has since heard; Bismarck was one of them. I have eaten smoked goose with him in Pommern. You see, I am very old, very old. I have spent my life solving a riddle. It is the same riddle that has balked you, my young friend. But I have striven for the solution; you have merely wailed against the riddle's existence."

Vane felt a flush of shame.

"True," he murmured, "true. I never went further into any art, any science, than to find its shortcomings."

"Yet even that," resumed the Professor, "is something. You are, at any rate, the only man for my purpose."

"Your purpose?"

"Yes. It is the same as yours. You are to be the instrument; I furnish the power. You are to be able to feel, to think, as others do."

"Oh!" muttered Vane, "impossible." Now that his wish was called possible of fulfilment, he shrank a little from it. He followed the Professor up a long flight of curving steps, through dim halls, to where a bluish light flickered. As they passed this feeble glow it flared suddenly into a brilliant jet of flame; a door swung open, revealing a somewhat bare chamber fitted up partly as a study, partly as a laboratory. The door closed behind them silently.

"Mere trickery," said the Professor, "the sort of thing that the knaves of science fool the world with. Will you sit down? Here is where I have worked for—for more years than you have lived, Mr. Vane. Here is where I have succeeded. In pursuit of this success I have spent my life and

arly all the fortune that my family made in generations gone. I have this house, and my
ughter, and my science. The world spins madly all about me, in this splendid town; here, in
s stillness, I have worked to make that world richer than I found it. Will you help me?"

Jane had flung himself upon a wicker couch. He watched his host striding up and down the
om with a fervor that had nothing of senility in it. The look of earnestness upon that fine old
:e was magnetic. Vane's mistrust vanished at sight of it.

'If you will trust me," he answered. He saw himself as the beneficiary, his host as the giver of a
:at gift.

'I trust you. I heard enough, to-night, to believe you sincere in wishing to see life from another
il than your own. But you must promise to obey my instructions to the letter."

I promise."

\ sense of farce caught Vane. "And now," he said, "what is it? A powder I must swallow, or a
ice you pass me into, or what?"

'he professor shook his head gravely. "It is none of those things. It is much simpler. I should
: wonder but that the ancients knew it. But human life is so much more complex now; the
)eriences you will gain will be larger than they could ever have been in other ages. Do you
.lize what I am about to give you? The power to take upon you the soul of another, just as an
or puts on the outer mask of another! And I ask for no reward. Simply the joy of seeing my
)cess active; and afterwards, perhaps, to give my secret to the world. But you are to enjoy it
ne, first. Of course—there may be risks. Do you take them?"

I do," said Vane.

Ie could hear the whistling of steamers out in the harbor, and the noise of the great town came
him faintly. All that seemed strangely remote. His whole intelligence was centered upon his
st, upon the sparsely furnished room, and the secret whose solution he thought himself
)roaching. He was, for almost the first time in his life, intense in the mere act of existence; he
s conscious of no imitation of others; his analysis of self was sunk in an eagerness, a tenseness
purposeness hitherto unfelt.

'he professor went to a far, dark corner of the room, and rolled thence a tall, sheeted thing that
ght have been a painting, or an easel. He held it tenderly; his least motion with it revealed
icitude. When it was immediately in front of where Vane reclined, Vanlief loosed his hold of
: thing, and began pacing up and down the room.

'The question of mirrors," he began, after what seemed to Vane an age, "has never, I suppose,
erested you."

On the contrary," said Vane, "I have had Italy searched for the finest of its cheval-glasses. In
' dressing-room are several that would give even a man of your fine height, sir, a complete
lection of every detail, from a shoe-lace to an eyebrow. It is not altogether vanity; but I never
ild do justice to my toilette before a mirror that showed me only a shoulder, or a waist, or a
)t, at a time; I want the full-length portrait or nothing. I like to see myself as others will see
:; not in piece-meal. The Florentines made lovely mirrors."

They did." Vanlief smiled sweetly. "Yet I have made a better." He paced the floor again, and then resumed speech. "I am glad you like tall mirrors. You will have learned how careful one must be of them. One more or less in your dressing-room will not matter, eh?"

"I have an excellent man," said Vane. "There has not been a broken mirror in my house for years. He looks after them as if they were his own."

"Ah, better and better."

Vane interrupted the Professor's silence with, "It is a mirror, then?"

"Yes," said Vanlief, nodding at the sheeted mirror, "it is a mirror. Have you ever thought of the wonderfulness of mirrors? What wonder, and yet what simplicity! To think that I—I, a simple, plodding old man of science—should be the only one to have come upon the magic of a mirror!" His talk took the note of monologue. He was pacing, pacing, pacing; smiling at Vane now and then, and fingering the covered mirror with loving touch as he passed near it. "Have you ever, as a child, looked into a mirror in the twilight, and seen there another face beside your own? Have you never thought that to the mirror were revealed more things than the human eye can note? Have you heard of the old, old folk-superstitions; of the bride that may not see herself in a mirror without tragedy touching her; of the Warwickshire mirror that must be covered in a house of death, lest the corpse be seen in it; of the future that some magic mirrors could reveal? Fanciful tales, all of them; yet they have their germ of truth, and for my present discovery I owe them something." He drew the sheet from the mirror, and revealed another veil of gauze resting upon the glass, as, in some houses, the most prized pictures are sometimes doubly covered. "You see; it is just a mirror, a full-length mirror. But, oh, my dear Vane, the wonderfulness of this mirror! I have only to look into this mirror; to veil it; and then, when next you glance into it, if it be within the hour, my soul, my spirit, my very self, passes from the face of the mirror to you! That is the whole secret, or at least, the manifestation of it! Do you wish to be the President, to think his thoughts, feel as he feels, dream as he dreams? He has only to look into this mirror, and you have only to take from it, as one plucks a lily from the pool, the spiritual image he has left there! Think of it, Vane, think of it! Is this not seeing life? Is this not riddling the secret of existence? To reach the innermost depths of another's spirit; to put on his soul, as others can put on your clothes, if you left them on a chair,—is this not a stupendous thing?" In his fever and fervor the professor had exhausted his strength; he flung himself into a chair. Vane saw the old man's eyes glowing and his chest throbbing with passion; he hardly knew whether the whole scene was real or a something imposed upon his senses by a species of hypnotism. He passed his hand before his forehead; he shook his head. Yet nothing changed. Vanlief, in the chair, still quaking with excitement; the mirror, veiled and immobile.

For a time the room stood silent, save for Vanlief's heavy breathing.

"Of course," he resumed presently, in a quieter tone, "you cannot be expected to believe, until you have tried. But trial is the easiest thing in the world. I can teach you the mere externals to be observed in five minutes. One trial will convince you. After that,—my dear Vane, you have the gamut of humanity to go. You can be another man every day. No secret of any human heart will be a secret to you. All wisdom can be gained by you; all knowledge, all thought, can be yours. Oh, Orson Vane, I wonder if you realize your fortune! Or—is it possible that you withdraw?"

Jane got up resolutely.

"No," he said, "I have faith—at last. I am with you, heart and soul. Life seems splendid to me, the first time. When can I have the mirror taken to my house?"

CHAPTER IV.

Vane's dressing-room was a tasteful chamber, cool and light. Its walls, its furniture, and its hangings told of a wide range of interest. There was nowhere any obvious bias; the æsthetic was no more insistent than the sporting. Orson Vane loved red-haired women as Henner painted them, and he played the aristocratic waltzes of Chopin; but he also valued the cruel breaking-bit that he had brought home from Texas, and read the racing-column in the newspaper quite as carefully as he did the doings of his society. Some hint of this diversity of tastes showed in this, the most intimate room of his early mornings. There were some of those ruddy British prints that are now almost depressingly conventional with men of sporting habits; signed photographs of more or less prominent and personable personages were scattered pell-mell. All the chairs and lounges were of wicker; so much so that some of the men who hobnobbed with Vane declared that a visit to his dressing-room was as good as a yachting cruise.

The morning was no longer young. On the avenue the advance guard of the fashionable assault upon the shopping district was already astir. The languorous heat that reflects from the town's asphalt was gaining in power momentarily.

Orson Vane, fresh from a chilling, invigorating bath, a Japanese robe of exquisite coolness his only covering, sat regarding an addition to his furniture. It had come while he slept. It was proof that the adventure of the night had not been a mere figment of his dreams.

He touched a bell. To the man who answered the call, he said:

"Nevins, I have bought a new mirror. You are to observe a few simple rules in regard to this mirror. In the first place, to avoid confusion, it is always to be called the New Mirror. Is that plain?

"Quite so, sir."

"I may have orders to give about it, or notes to send, or things of that sort, and I want no mistakes made. In the next place, the cord that uncovers the mirror is never to be pulled, never to be touched, save at my express order. Not—under any circumstances. I do not wish the mirror used. Have you any curiosity left, Nevins?"

"None, sir."

"So much the better. In Lord Keswick's time, I think, you still had a touch of that vice, curiosity. Your meddling got you into something of a scrape. Do you remember?"

"Oh, sir," said the man, with a little gesture of shame and pain, "you didn't need reminding me. Have I ever forgotten your saving me from that foolishness?"

"You're right, Nevins; I think I can trust you. But this is a greater trust than any of the others. A great deal depends; mark that; a very great deal. It is not an ordinary mirror, this one; not one of the others compares with it; it is the gem of my collection. Not a breath is to touch it, save as I command."

"I'll see to it, sir."

"Any callers, Nevins?"

"Mr. Moncreith, sir, looked in, but left no word. And the postman."

No duns, Nevins?"

Not in person, sir."

Dear me! Is my position on the wane? When a man is no longer dunned his credit is either too
od or too bad; or else his social position is declining." He picked up the tray with the letters,
ı his eye over them quickly, and said, "Thank the stars; they still dun me by post. There should
a law against it; yet it is as sweet to one's vanity as an angry letter from a woman. Nevins, is
: day dull or garish?"

It's what I should call bright, sir."

Then you may lay out some gloomy clothes for me. I would not add to the heat wittingly.
d, Nevins!"

Yes sir."

If anyone calls before I breakfast, unless it happens to be Professor Vanlief,—Vanlief,
vins, of the Vanliefs of New Amsterdam—say I am indisposed."

Ie dressed himself leisurely, thinking of the wonderful adventures into living that lay before
ɔ. He rehearsed the simple instructions that Vanlief had given him the night before. It was all
erly simple. As one looked into the mirror, the spirit of that one lay on the surface, waiting for
next person that glanced that way. There followed a complete exodus of the spirit from the
ɔ body into the other. The recipient was himself plus the soul of the other. The exodus left that
ier in a state something like physical collapse. There would be, for the recipient of the new
rsonality, a sense of double consciousness; the mind would be like a palimpsest, the one will
d the one habit imposed upon the other. The fact that the person whose spirit passed from him
ɔn the magic mirror was left more or less a wreck was cause for using the experiment charily,
the Professor took pains to warn Orson. There was a certain risk. The mirror might be broken;
ɔ could never tell. It would be better to pick one's subjects wisely, always with a definite
rpose. This man might be used to teach that side of life; that man another. It was not a thing to
· with. It was to be played with as little as human life itself. Vivisection was a pastime to this;
; implicated the spirit, the other only the body.

Consideration of the new avenues opening for his intelligence had already begun to alter
ne's outlook on life. Persons who remarked him, a little later, strolling the avenue, wondered
he brilliance of his look. He seemed suddenly sprayed with a new youth, a new enthusiasm. It
s not, as some of his conversations of that morning proved, an utter lapse into optimism on his
t; but it was an exchange of the mere passive side of pessimism for its healthier, more buoyant
e. He was able to smile to himself as he met the various human marionettes of the avenue; the
rsons whose names you would be sure to read every Sunday in the society columns, and who
ɛmed, consequently, out of place in any more aristocratic air. He bowed to the newest beauty,
waved a hand to the most perennial of the faded beaux. The vociferous attire of the actors,
ɔ idled conspicuously before the shop-windows, caused him inward shouts of laughter; a day
so ago the same sight would have embittered his hour for him.

\t Twenty-third street something possessed him to patronize one of the Sicilian flower-sellers.
e man had, happily, not importuned him; he merely held his wares, and waited, mutely. Orson

put a sprig of lily-of-the-valley into his coat.

Before he left his rooms he had spent an hour or so writing curt notes to the smartest addresses in town. All his invitations were declined by him; a trip to Cairo, he had written, would keep him from town for some time. He took this ruse because he felt that the complications of his coming experiment might be awkward; it was as well to pave the way. Certainly he could not hope to fulfil his social obligations in the time to come. An impression that he was abroad was the best way out of the dilemma. The riddance from fashionable duties added to his gaiety; he felt like a school-boy on holiday.

It was in this mood that he saw, on the other side of the avenue, a figure that sent a flush to his skin. There was no mistaking that wonderful hair; in the bright morning it shone with a glow a trifle less garish than under the electric light, but it was the same, the same. To make assurance surer, there, just under the hat—a hat that no mere male could have expressed in phrases, a thing of gauze and shimmer—lay a spray of lilies-of-the-valley. The gown—Vane knew at a glance that it was a beautiful gown and a happy one, though as different as possible from the filmy thing she had worn when first he saw her, in the mirror, at night.

At first unconsciously, and then with quite brazen intent, he found himself keeping pace, on his side of the street, with the girl opposite. He knew not what emotion possessed him; no hint of anything despicable came to him; he had forgotten himself utterly, and he was merely following some sweet, blind impulse. Orson Vane was a man who had tasted the froth and dregs of his town no less thoroughly than other men; there were few sensations, few emotions, he had not tried. Almost the only sort of woman he did not know was The woman. In the year of his majority he had made a summer of it on the Sound in his steam yacht, and his enemies declared that all the harbors he had anchored in were left empty of both champagne and virtue. Yet not even his bitterest enemy had ever accused him of anything vulgar, brazen, coarse, conspicuous.

Luke Moncreith was a friend of Vane's, there was no reason for doubting that. But even he experienced a little shock when he met Vane, was unseen of him, and was then conscious, in a quick turn of the head, that Vane's eyes, his entire vitality, were upon a woman's figure across the avenue.

"The population of the Bowery, of Forty-second street, and of the Tenderloin," said Moncreith to himself, "have a name for that sort of thing." He clicked his tongue upon his teeth once or twice. "Poor Orson! Is it the beginning of the end? Last night he seemed a little mad. Poor Orson!" Then, with furtive shame at his bad manners, he turned about and watched the two. Even at that distance the sunlight glowed like a caress upon the hair of her whom Orson followed. "The girl," exclaimed Moncreith, "the girl of the mirror." He came to a halt before a photographer's window, the angle of which gave him a view of several blocks behind.

Orson Vane, in the meanwhile, was as if there was but one thing in life for him: a meeting with this radiant creature with the lilies. Once he thought he caught a sidelong glance of hers; a little smile even hovered an instant upon her lips; yet, at that distance, he could not be sure. None of the horrible things occurred to him as possibilities; that she might be an adventuress, or a mere masquerading shop-girl, or an adroit soubrette. No tangible intention came to the young man; he

d not made it clear to himself whether he would keep on, and on, and on, until she came to her
n door; whether he would accost her; whether he would leave all to chance; or whether he
uld fashion circumstances to his end.

he girl turned into a little bookshop that, as it happened, was one of Vane's familiar haunts. It
s a place where one could always find the new French and German things, and where the
ipman was not a mere instrument for selling whatever rubbish publishers chose to shoot at the
blic. When Vane entered he found this shopman, who nodded smilingly at him, busy with a
irded German. The girl stood at a little table, passing her slim fingers lovingly over the titles
the books that lay there. It was evident that she had no wish for advice from the assistant who
vered in the background. She did not so much as glance at him. Her eyes were all for her
inds in print. She did look up, the veriest trifle, it is true, when Orson came in; it was so swift,
shy a look that he, in a mist of emotions, could not have sworn to it. As for him, a boyish
dness took him to the other side of the table at which she stood; he bent over the books, and
hands almost touched her fingers. In that little, quiet nook, he became, all of a moment, once
ire a youth of twenty; he felt the first shy stirrings of tenderness, of worship. The names of the
iumes swam for him in a mere haze. He saw nothing save only the little figure before him, the
mmer of rose upon her face passing into the ruddier shimmer of her hair; the perfume of her
es and some yet subtler scent, redolent of fairest linen, most fragile laces and the utterest
rity, came over him like a glow.

nd then the marvel, the miracle of her voice!

Oh, Mr. Vane," he heard her saying, "do help me!" Their eyes met and he was conscious of a
vildering beauty in hers; it was with quite an effort that he did not, then and there, do
nething absurd and stupid. His hesitation, his astonishment, cost him a second or so; before he
ight his composure again, she was explaining, sweetly, plaintively, "Help me to make up my
nd. About a book."

Why did you add that?" he asked, his wits sharp now, and his voice still a little unsteady.
here are so many other things I would like to help you in. A book? What sort of a book? One
those stories where the men are all eight feet high, and wear medals, and the women are all
idels for Gibson? Or one of those aristocratic things where nobody is less than a prince, except
inevitable American, who is a newspaper man and an abomination? Or is it, by any chance,"
paused, and dropped his voice, as if he were approaching a dreadful disclosure, "poetry?"
he shook her head. The lilies in her hair nodded, and her smile came up like a radiance in that
k little corner. And, oh, the music in her laugh! It blew ennui away as effectually as a storm
irls away a leaf.

No," she said, "it is none of those things. I told you I had not made up my mind."
It is a thing you should never attempt. Making up the mind is a temptation only the bravest of
can resist. One should always delegate the task to someone else."

he girl frowned gently. "If it is the fashion to talk like that," she said, "I do not want to be in
fashion."

Ie took the rebuke with a laugh. "It is hard," he pleaded, "to keep out of the fashion.

Everything we do is a fashion of one sort or another." He glanced at her wonderful hat, at the gown that held her so closely, so tenderly. "I am sure you are in the fashion," he said.

"If Mr. Orson Vane tells me so, I must believe it," she answered. "But I wear only what suits me; if the fashion does not suit me, I avoid the fashion."

"But you cannot avoid beauty," he urged, "and to be fair is always the fashion."

She turned her eyes to him full of reproach. They said, as plainly as anything, "How crude! How stupidly obvious!" As if she had really spoken, he went on, in plain embarassment:

"I beg your pardon. I—I am very silly this morning. Something has gone to my head. I really don't think I'd better advise you about anything to read. I—"

"Oh," she interrupted, already full of forgiveness, since it was not in her nature to be cruel for more than a moment at a time, "but you must. I am really desperate. All I ask is that you do not urge a fashionable book, a book of the day, or a book that should be in the library of every lady. I am afraid of those books. They are like the bores one turns a corner to avoid."

"You make advice harder and harder. Is it possible you really want a book to read, rather than to talk about?"

"I really do," she admitted, "I told you I had no thought about the fashion."

"You are like a figure from the Middle Ages," he said, "with your notion about books."

"Am I so very wrinkled?" she asked. She put her hand to her veil, with a gesture of solicitous inquiry. "To be young," she sighed, with a pout, "and yet to seem old. I am quite a tragedy."

"A goddess," he murmured, "but not of tragedy." He laughed sharply, and took a book from the table, using it to keep his eyes from the witchery of her as he continued: "Don't you see why I'm talking such nonsense? If it meant prolonging the glimpse of you, there's no end, simply no end, to the rubbish I could talk!"

"And no beginning," she put in, "to your sincerity."

"Oh, I don't know. One still has fits and starts of it! There's no telling what might not be done; it might come back to one, like childishness in old age." He put down the book, and looked at her in something like appeal. "There is such a thing as a sincerity one is ashamed of, that one hides, and disguises, and that the world refuses to see. The world? The world always means an individual. In this case the world is—"

"The world is yours, like Monte Cristo," she interposed, "how embarassed you must feel. The responsibility must be enervating! I have always thought the clever thing for Monte Cristo to have done was to lose the world; to hide it where nobody could find it again." She tapped her boot with her parasol, charmingly impatient. "I suppose," she sighed, "I shall have to ask that stupid clerk for a book, after all. He looks as if he would far rather sell them by weight."

"No, no, I couldn't allow that. Consider me all eagerness to aid you. Is it to be love, or ghosts, or laughter?"

"Love and laughter go well together," she said. "I want a book I can love and laugh with, not at."

"I know," he nodded. "The tear that makes the smile come after. You want something charming, something sweet, something that will taste pleasantly no matter how often you read it.

rifle, and yet—a treasure. Such a book as, I dare say, every writer dreams of doing once in his
; the sort of book that should be bound in rose-leaves. And you expect me to betray a treasure
e that to you? And my reward? But no, I beg your pardon; I have my reward now, and here,
l the debt is still mine. I can merely put you in the way of a printed page; while you—" He
pped, roving for the right word. His eyes spoke what his voice could not find. He finished,
ely, and yet aptly enough, "You—are you."

I don't believe," she declared, with the most arch elevation of the darkest eyebrows, "that you
ow one book from another. You are an impostor. You are sparring for time. I have given you
much time as it is. I am going." She picked up her skirts with one slim hand, turned on a tiny
l, and looked over her shoulder with an air, a mischievousness, that made Orson ache, yes,
ply ache with curiosity about her. He put out a hand in expostulation.

Please," he pleaded, "please don't go. I have found the book. I really have. But you must take
word for it. You mustn't open it till you are at home." He handed it to the clerk to be wrapped
. "And now," he went on, "won't you tell me something? I—upon my honor, I can't think
ere we met?"

One hardly expects Mr. Orson Vane to remember all the young women in society," she
iled. "Besides, if I must confess: I am only just what society calls 'out.' I have seen Mr. Orson
ne: but he has not seen me. Mr. Vane is a leader; I am—" She shrugged her shoulder, raised
eyebrows, pursed up her mouth, oh, to a complete gesture that was the prettiest, most
vildering finish to any sentence ever uttered.

Oh," said Orson, "but you are mistaken. I have seen you. No longer ago than last night. In—"

In a mirror," she laughed. Then she grew suddenly quite solemn. "Oh, you mustn't think I
n't know who you were. It was all very rash of me, and very improper, my speaking to you,
t now, but—"

It was very sweet," he interposed.

But," she went on, not heeding his remark at all, "I knew you so well by sight, and I had really
n introduced to you once,—one of a bevy of debutantes, merely an item in a chorus—and,
ides, my father—"

Your father?" repeated Orson, jogging his memory, "you don't mean to say—"

My father is Augustus Vanlief," she said.

Ie took a little time to digest the news. The clerk handed him the book and the change. He
v, now, whence that charm, that grace, that beauty came; he recalled that the late Mrs. Vanlief
l been one of the Waddells; there was no better blood in the country. With the name, too, there
ne the thought of the wonderful revelations that were presently to come to him, thanks to this
l's father. A sort of dizziness touched him: he felt a quick conflict between the wish to worship
s girl, and the wish to probe deeper into life. It was with a very real effort that he brushed the
rm of her from him, and relapsed, again, into the man who meant to know more of human life
n had ever been known before.

Ie took out a silver pencil and held it poised above the book.

This book," he said, "is for you, you know, not for your father. Your father and I are to be great friends but—I want to be friends, also, with—" he looked a smiling appeal, "with—whom?"

"With Miss Vanlief," she replied, mockingly. "My other name? I hate it; really I do. Perhaps my father will tell you."

She had given him the tip of her fingers, her gown had swung perfume as it followed her, and she was out and away before he could do more than give her the book, bow her good-bye, and stand in amaze at her impetuousness, her verve. The thought smote him that, on the night before, he had seen her, in the mirror, and spurned the notion of her being other than a sham, a mockery. How did he know, even now, that she was other than that? Yet, what had happened to him that he had been able so long to stay under her charm, to believe in her, to wish for her, to feel that she was hardly mortal, but some strange, sweet, splendid dream? Was he the same man who, only a few hours ago, had held himself shorn of all the primal emotions? He beat these questionings back and forth in his mind; now doubting himself, now doubting this girl. Surely she had not, in that dining-room, been sitting with her father? Would he not have seen them together? Perhaps she was with some of her family's womenfolk? Yes; now he remembered; she had been at a table with several other ladies, all elderly. He wished he knew the name one might call her, if ... if....

Luke Moncreith came into the shop. Orson caught a shadow of a frown on the other's face. Moncreith's voice was sharp and bitter when he spoke.

"Been buying the shop?" he asked.

"No," said Orson, in some wonder. "Only one book."

"Hope you'll like it," said the other, with a manner that meant the very opposite.

"I? Oh, I read it ages ago. It was for somebody else. You seem very curious about it?"

"I am. You aren't usually the man to dawdle in bookshops."

"Dawdle?" Orson turned on the other sharply. "What the deuce do you mean? Are you my keeper, or what? If I choose to, I can live in this shop, can't I?"

"Oh, Lord, yes! Looks odd, just the same, you trailing in here after a petticoat, and hanging around for—" he pulled out his watch,—"for a good half hour."

Orson burst out in a sort of clenched breath of rage. He kept the phrases down with difficulty. "Better choose your words," he said. "I don't like your words, and your watch be damned. Since when have my—my friends taken to timing my actions? It's a blessing I'm going abroad."

He turned and walked out of the shop, fiercely, swiftly. As the fresh air struck his face, he put his hand to it, and shook his head, wonderingly. "What's the matter with Moncreith? With me?" He thought of the title of the book he had just given away. "Are we all as mad as that?" he asked himself.

The title was "March Hares."

CHAPTER V.

A young man so prominent in the town as Orson Vane had naturally a very large list of acquaintances. He knew, in the fashionable phrase, "everybody," and "everybody" knew him. His acquaintances ranged beyond the world of fashion; the theatre, the turf, and many other regions had denizens who knew Orson Vane and held him in esteem. He had always lived a careful, well-mannered life; his name had never been in the newspapers save in the inescapable columns touching society.

When he was ready to proceed with the experiment of the mirror, the largeness of his social register was at once a pleasure and a pain. There were so many, so many! It was evident that he must use the types most promising in eccentricity; he must adventure forth in company with the strangest souls, not the mere ordinary ones.

Sitting in the twilight of his rooms one day, it occurred to him that he was now ripe for his first decision. Whose soul should he seize? That was the question. He had spent a week or so perfecting plans, stalling off awkward episodes, schooling his servants. There was no telling what might not happen.

He picked up a newspaper. A name caught his eye; he gave a little laugh.

"The very man!" he told himself, "the very man. Society's court fool; it will be worth something to know what lies under his cap and bells."

He scrawled a note, enclosed it, and rang for Nevins.

"Have that taken, at once, to Mr. Reginald Hart. And then, presently, have a hansom called and let it wait nearby."

"Reggie will be sure to come," he said, when alone. "I've told him there was a pretty woman here."

He felt a nervous restlessness. He paced his room, fingering the frames of his prints, trying the hood of his new mirror, adjusting the blinds of the windows. He tingled with mental and physical expectation. He wondered whether nothing, after all, would be the result. How insane it was to expect any such thing to happen as Vanlief had vapored of! This was the twentieth century rather than the tenth; miracles never happened. Yet how fervently he wished for one! To feel the soul of another superimposing itself upon his own; to know that he had committed the grandest larceny under heaven, the theft of a soul, and to gain, thereby, complete insight into the spiritual machinery of another mortal!

Nevins returned, within a little time, bringing word that Mr. Hart had been found at home, and would call directly.

Vane pushed the new mirror to a position where it would face the door. He told Nevins not to enter the room after Mr. Hart; to let him enter, and let the curtain fall behind him.

He took up a position by a window and waited. The minutes seemed heavy as lead. The air was unnaturally still.

At last he heard Nevins, in gentle monosyllables. Another voice, high almost to falsetto, crashed against the stillness.

Then the curtain swung back.

Reginald Hart, whom all the smart world never called other than Reggie Hart, stood for a moment in the curtain-way, the mirror barring his path. He caught his image there to the full, the effeminate, full face, the narrow-waisted coat, the unpleasantly womanish hips. He put out his right hand, as if groping in the dark. Then he said, shrilly, stammeringly.

"Vane! Oh, Vane, where the de—"

He sank almost to his knees. Vane stepping forward, caught him by the shoulder and put him into an arm-chair. Hart sat there, his head hunched between his shoulders.

"Silly thing to do, Vane, old chappy. Beastly sorry for this—stunt of mine. Too many tea-parties lately, Vane, too much dancing, too much—" his voice went off into a sigh. "Better get a cab," he said, limply.

He had quite forgotten why he had come: he was simply in collapse, mentally and physically. Vane, trembling with excitement and delight, walked up to the mirror from behind and sent the veil upon its face again. Then he had Nevins summon the cab. He watched Hart tottering out, upon Nevins' shoulder, with a dry, forced smile.

So it was real! He could hardly believe it. In seconds, in the merest flash, his visitor had faded like a flower whose root is plucked. The man had come in, full of vitality, quite, in fact, himself; he had gone out a mere husk, a shell.

But there was still the climax ahead. Had he courage for it, now that it loomed imminent? Should he send for Hart and have him pick up his soul where he had dropped it? Or should he, stern in his first purpose, fit that soul upon his own, as one fits a glove upon the hand? There was yet time. It depended only upon whether Hart or himself faced the mirror when the veil was off.

He cut his knot of indecision sharply, with a stride to the mirror, a jerk at the cord and a steady gaze into the clear pool of light, darkened only by his own reflection.

Strain his eyes as he would, he could feel no change, not the faintest stir of added emotion. He let the curtain drop upon the mirror listlessly.

Walking to his window-seat again, he was suddenly struck by his image in one of the other glasses. He was really very well shaped; he felt a wish to strip to the buff; it was rather a shame to clothe limbs as fine as those. He was quite sure there were friends of his who would appreciate photographs of himself, in some picturesque costume that would hide as little as possible. It was an age since he had any pictures taken. He called for Nevins. His voice struck Nevins as having a taint of tenor in it.

"Nevins," he said, "have the photographer call to-morrow, like a good man, won't you? You know, the chap, I forget his name, who does all the smart young women. I'll be glad to do the fellow a service; do him no end of good to have his name on pictures of me. I'm thinking of something a bit startling for the Cutter's costume ball, Nevins, so have the man from Madame Boyer's come for instructions. And see if you can find me some perfume at the chemist's; something heavy, Nevins. The perfumes at once, that's a dear man. I want them in my pillows tonight."

When the man was gone, his master went to the sideboard, opened it, and gave a gentle sigh of appointment.

Careless of me," he murmured, "to have no Red Ribbon in the place. How can any gentleman ord to be without it? Dear, dear, if any of the girls and boys had caught me without it. Another ng I must tell Nevins. Nothing but whisky! Abominably vulgar stuff! Can't think, really, 'pon nor I can't, how I ever came to lay any of it in. And no cigarettes in the place. Goodness me! nat sweet cigarettes those are Mrs. Barrett Weston always has! Wonder if that woman will ask ; to her cottage this summer."

Ie strolled to the window, yawned, stretched out his arms, drawing his hands towards him at : end of his gesture. He inspected the fingers minutely. They needed manicuring. He began to t down a little list of things to be done. He strolled over to the tabouret where invitations lay ittered all about. That dear Mrs. Sclatersby was giving a studio-dance; she was depending on n for a novel feature. Perhaps if he did a little skirt-dance. Yes; the notion pleased him. He uld sit down, at once, and write a hint to a newspaper man who would be sure to make a isation of this skirt-dance.

That done, he heard Nevins knocking.

Oh," he murmured, "the perfumes. So sweet!" He buried his nose in a handful of the sachet-gs. He sprayed some Maria Farina on his forehead. Perfumes, he considered, were worth rship just as much as jewels or music. The more sinful a perfume seemed, the more nulating it was to the imagination. Some perfumes were like drawings by Beardsley.

Ie looked at the walls. He really must get some Beardsleys put up. There was nothing like a ardsley for jogging a sluggish fancy; if you wanted to see everything that milliners and ssmakers existed by hiding, all you had to do was to sup sufficiently on Beardsley. He ught of inventing a Beardsley cocktail; if he could find a mixture that would make the brain te pagan, he would certainly give it that name.

Iis mind roved to the feud between the Montagues and Capulets of the town. It was one of se modern feuds, made up of little social frictions, infinitesimal jealousies, magnified by a licious press into a national calamity. It was a feud, he told himself, that he would have to nd. It would mean, for him, the lustre from both houses. And there was nothing, in the smart rld, like plenty of lustre. There were several sorts of lustre: that of money, of birth, and of blic honors. Personally, he cared little for the origin of his lustre; so it put him in the very efront of smartness he asked for nothing more. Of course, his own position was quite peccable. The smart world might narrow year by year; the Newport set, and the Millionaire , and the Knickerbocker set—they might all dwindle to one small world of smartness; yet hing that could happen could keep out an Orson Vane. The name struck him, as it shaped :lf in his mind, a trifle odd. An Orson Vane? Yes, of course, of course. For that matter, who l presumed to doubt the position of a Vane? He asked himself that, with a sort of defiance. An son Vane, an Orson Vane? He repeated the syllables over and over, in a whisper at first, and n aloud, until the shrillness of his tone gave him a positive start.

Ie rang the bell for Nevins.

Nevins," he said, and something in him fought against his speech, "tell me, that's a good man,—is there anything, anything wrong with—me?"

"Nothing sir," said Nevins stolidly.

Orson Vane gave a sort of gasp as the man withdrew. It had come to him suddenly; the under-self was struggling beneath the borrowed self. He was Orson Vane, but he was also another.

Who? What other?

He gave a little shrill laugh as he remembered. Reggie Hart,—that was it,—Reggie Hart.

He sat down to undress for sleep. He slipped into bed as daintily as a woman, nestling to the perfumed pillows.

Nevins, in his part of the house, sat shaking his head. "If he hadn't given me warning," he told himself, "I'd have sent for a doctor."

CHAPTER VI.

The smart world received the change in Orson Vane with no immediate wonder. Wonder is, at outset, a vulgarity; to let nothing astonish you is part of a smart education. A good many of smartest hostesses in town were glad that Vane had emerged from his erstwhile air of stocratic aloofness; he took, with them, the place that Reggie Hart's continuing illness left cant.

n the regions where Vane had been actually intimate whispers began to go about, it is true, and vas with no little difficulty that an occasional story about him was kept out of the gossipy ges of the papers. Vane was constantly busy seeking notoriety. His attentions to several of the unger matrons were conspicuous. Yet he was so much of a stimulating force, in a society ere passivity was the rule, that he was welcome everywhere.

Ie had become the court fool of the smart set.

'o him, the position held nothing degrading. It was, he argued, a reflection on smart society, her on himself, that, to be prominent in it, one must needs wear cap and bells. Moreover his ition allowed him, now and then, the utterance of grim truths that would not have been ened to from anyone not wearing the jester's license.

\t the now famous dinner given by Mrs. Sclatersby, Orson Vane seized a lull in the nversation, by remarking, in his ladylike lisp:

My dear Mrs. Sclatersby, I have such a charming idea. I am thinking of syndicating myself."

Mrs. Sclatersby put up her lorgnettes and smiled encouragement at Orson. "It sounds Wall eety," she said, "you're not going to desert us, are you?"

Oh, nothing so dreadful. It would be an entirely smart syndicate, you know; a syndicate of ich you would be a member. I sometimes think, you know, that I do not distribute myself to best advantage. There have been little jealousies, now and then, have there not?" He looked, a bird-like, perky way, at Mrs. Barrett Weston, and the only Mrs. Carlos. "I have been unable be in two places at once. Now a syndicate—a syndicate could arrange things so that there uld be no disappointments, no clashings of engagements, no waste of opportunity.

How clever you always are," said a lady at Orson's right. She had chameleon hair, and her ise was that of a soubrette. The theatre was tremendously popular as a society model that son. Orson blew a kiss at her, and went on with his speech.

Actors do it, you know. Painters have done it. Inventors do it. Why not I?" He paused to ble an olive. "To contribute to the gaiety of our little world is, after all, the one thing worth ile. Think how few picturesque people we have! Eccentricity is terribly lacking in the town. e have no Whistler; Mansfield is rather a dull imitation. Of course there is George Francis in; but he is a trifle, a trifle too much of the larger world, don't you think?"

I never saw the man in my life," asserted the hostess.

Exactly," said Orson, "he makes himself too cheap. It keeps us from seeing him. But Whistler; nk of Whistler, in New York! He would wear a French hat, fight duels every day, lampoon a tic every hour, and paint nocturnes on the Fifth avenue pavement! He would make Diana fall from the Tower in sheer envy. He would go through the Astoria with monocle and mockery, and smile blue peacock smiles at Mr. Blashfield and Mr. Simmons. He would etch himself upon the town. We would never let him go again. We need that sort of thing. Our ambitions and our patience are cosmopolitan; but we lack the public characters to properly give fire and color to our streets. Now I—"

He let his eyes wander about the room, a delicate smile of invitation on his lips.

"Don't you think," said one of the ladies, "that you are quite—quite bohemian enough?"

Orson shuddered obviously. "My dear lady," he urged, "it is a dreadful thing to be bohemian. It is no longer smart. If I am considered the one, I cannot possibly be the other. There is, to be sure, a polite imitation; but it is quite an art to imitate the thing with just sufficient indolence. But I really wish you would think the thing over, Mrs. Sclatersby. I know nobody who would do the thing better than I. Our men are mostly too fond of fashion, and too afraid of fancy. One must not be ashamed of being called foolish. Whistler uses butterflies; somebody else used sunflowers and green carnations; I should use—lilies, I think, lilies-of-the-valley. Emblematic of the pure folly of my pose, you know. One must do something like that, you see, to gain smart applause; impossible hats and improbable hair, except in the case of actresses, are quite extinct."

A Polish orchestra that had been hitherto unsuccessful against the shrill monologue of Orson, and the occasional laughter of the ladies, now sent out a sudden, fierce stream of melody. It was evident that they did not mean to take the insult of a large wage without offering some stormy moments in exchange. The diners assumed a patient air, eating in an abstracted manner, as if their stomachs were the only members of their bodies left unstunned by the music. The assemblage wore, in its furtive gluttony, an air of being in a plot of the most delicious danger. Some rather dowdy anecdotes went about in whispers, and several of the ladies made passionate efforts to blush. Orson Vane took a sip of some apricotine, explaining to his neighbor that he took it for the color; it was the color of verses by Verlaine. She had never heard of the man. Ah; then of course Mallarmé, and Symons and Francis Saltus were her gods? No; she said she liked Madame Louise; hers were by far the most fragile hats purchasable; what was the use of a hat if it was not fragile; to wear one twice was a crime, and to give one away unless it was decently crushed was an indiscretion. Orson quite agreed with her. To his other neighbor he confided that he was thinking of writing a book. It would be something entirely in the key of blue. He was busy explaining its future virtues, when an indiscreet lull came in the orchestral tornado.

"I mean to bring the pink of youth to the sallowest old age," he was saying, "and every page is to be as dangerous as a Bowery cocktail."

Then the storm howled forth again. Everyone talked to his or her neighbor at top voice. Now and then pauses in the music left fag ends of conversation struggling about the room.

"The decadents are simply the people who refuse to write twaddle for the magazines...."

"The way to make a name in the world is to own a soap factory and ape William Morris on the side...."

"I can always tell when it is Spring by looking at the haberdashers' windows. To watch shirts and ties blooming is so much nicer than flowers and those smelly things...."

The pleasantest things in the world all begin with a P. Powders, patches and poses—what
uld we do without them?..."

his sort of thing came out at loose ends now and then. Suddenly the music ceased altogether.
e diners all looked as if they had been caught in a crime. The lights went out in the room, and
re were little smothered shrieks. After an interval, a rosy glow lit up the conservatory beyond
palms; a little stage showed in the distance. Some notorious people from the music-halls
gan to do songs and dances, and offer comic monologues. The diners fell into a sort of
hargy. They did not even notice that Orson Vane's chair was empty.

/ane was in a little boudoir lent him by the hostess. His nostrils dilated with the perfume of her
t he felt everywhere. He sank into a silk-covered chair, before which he had arranged a full-
gth mirror, and several smaller glasses, with candles glowing all about him. He was conscious
a cloying sense of happiness over his physical perfections. He stripped garment after garment
m him with a care, a gentleness that argued his belief that haste was a foe to beauty. He
etched himself at full length, in epicurean enjoyment of himself. The flame of life, he told
nself, burnt the more steadily the less we wrapped it up. If we could only return to the pagan
!! And yet—what charm there was in dress! The body had, after all, a monotony, a sameness;
tenderest of its curves, the rosiest of its surfaces, must pall. But the infinite variety of clothes!
e delight of letting the most delicate tints of gauze caress the flesh, while to the world only the
erest stuffs were exposed! The rustle of fresh linen, the perfume that one could filter through
layers of one's attire!

)rson Vane closed his eyes, lazily, musingly. At that moment his proper soul was quite in
jection; the ecstasy in the usurping soul was all-powerful.

Ie was thinking of what the cheval-glass in that little room must have seen.

t would be unspeakably fine to be a mirror.

he little crystal clock ticking on the dressing-table tinkled an hour. It brought him from his
eries with a start. He began gliding into some shining, silken things of umber tints; they fitted
n to the skin.

Ie was a falconer.

t was a costume to strike pale the idlers at a bathing beach. There was not a crease, not a fold
where. A leathern thong upon a wrist, a feathered cap upon his head, were almost the only
nts that rose away from the body as God had fashioned it. Satisfaction filled him as he
veyed himself. But there was more to do. Above this costume he put the dress of a Spanish
een. When he lifted the massively brocaded train, there showed the most exquisitely chiseled
des, the promise of the most alluring legs. The corsage hinted a bust of the most soothing
tness. He spent fully ten minutes in happy admiration of his images in the mirrors.

Vhen he proceeded to the conservatory, it was by a secret corridor. The diners were wearily
tching a Frenchwoman who sang with her gloves, which were black and always on the point
falling down. She was very pathetic; she was trying to sing rag-time melodies because some
ot had told her the Newport set preferred that music. A smart young woman had danced a
ice of her own invention; everyone agreed, as they did about the man who paints with his toes,

that, considering her smartness in the fashionable world, it was not so much a wonder that she danced so well, as that she danced at all. They were quite sure the professional managers would offer her the most lavish sums; she would be quite as much of an attraction as the foreign peer who was trying to be a gentleman, where they are most needed, on the stage.

At a sign from Orson, the lights went out again, as the Frenchwoman finished her song. Several of the guests began to talk scandal in the dark; there are few occupations more fascinating than talking scandal in the dark. The question of whether it was better to be a millionaire or a fashionable and divorced beauty was beginning to agitate several people into almost violent argument, when the lights flared to the full.

The chorus of little "Ohs" and "Ahs," of rapid whispered comment, and of discreetly patted gloves, was quite fervid for so smart an assemblage. Except in the rarest cases, to gush is as fatal, in the smart world, as to be intolerant. There is a smart avenue between fervor and frowning; when you can find that avenue unconsciously, in the dark, as it were, you have little more to learn in the code of smartness.

Mrs. Sclatersby herself murmured, quite audibly:

"How sweet the dear boy looks!"

Her clan took the word up, and for a time the sibilance of it was like a hiss in the room. A man or two in the company growled out something that his fairer neighbor seemed unwilling to hear. These basso profundo sounds, if one could formulate them into words at all, seemed more like "Disgusting fool!" or "Sickening!" than anything else. But the company had very few men in it; in this, as in many other respects, the room resembled smart society itself. The smart world is engineered and peopled chiefly by the feminine element. The male sex lends to it only its more feminine side.

It is almost unnecessary to describe the picture that Orson Vane presented on that little stage. His beauty as "Isabella, Queen of Spain," has long since become public property; none of his later efforts in suppression of the many photographs that were taken, shortly after the Sclatersby dinner, have succeeded in quite expunging the portraits. At that time he gave the sittings willingly. He felt that these photographs represented the highest notch in his fame, the completest image of his ability to be as beautiful as the most beautiful woman.

Shame or nervousness was not part of Orson Vane's personality that night. He sat there, in the skillfully arranged scheme of lights, with his whole body attuned only to accurate impersonation of the character he represented. He got up. His motion, as he passed across the stage, was so utterly feminine, so made of the swaying, undulating grace that usually implies the woman; the gesture with his fan was so finically alluring; the poise of his head above his bared shoulders so coquettish,—that the women watching him almost held their breaths in admiration.

It was, you see, the most adroit flattery that a man could pay the entire sex of womankind.

Then the music, a little way off, began to strum a cachuca. The tempo increased; when finally the pace was something infectious, Orson Vane began a dance that remains, to this day, an episode in the annals of the smart. The vigor of his poses, the charm of his skirt-manipulation, carried the appreciation of his friends by storm. Some of the ladies really had hard work to keep

m rushing to the stage and kissing the young man then and there. When we are emotional, we
ıericans—to what lengths will we not go!

3ut the surprises were not yet over. A dash of darkness stayed the music; a swishing and a
pping came from the stage; then the lights. Vane stood, in statue position, as a falconer. You
ıld almost, under the umber silk, see the rippling of his veins.

)nly a second he stood so, but it was a second of triumph. The company was so agape with
nder, that there was no sound from it until the music and the bare stage, following a brief
iod of blackness, recalled it to its senses. Then it urged Mrs. Sclatersby to grant a great favor.
ſr. Vane must be persuaded not take off his falconer's costume; to mingle, for what little time
ıained, with the company without resuming his more conventional attire.

/ane smiled when the message came to him. He nodded his head. Then he sent for the
latersby butler.

Plenty of Red Ribbon!" he said to that person.

Plenty, sir."

Make a note of your commissions; a cheque in the morning."

hen he mingled again with his fellow-guests, and there was much toasting, and the bonds all
ısened a little, and the sparkle came up out of the glasses into the cheeks of the women. The
ıer men, one by one, took their way out.

Vomen crushed one another to touch the hero of the evening. Jealousies shot savage glances
)ut. Every increase in this emulation increased the love that Orson Vane felt for himself. He
essed a hand here, a lock there, with a king's condescension. If he felt a kiss upon his hand, he
iled a splendid, slightly wearied smile. If he had hot eyes turned on him, burning so fiercely as
spell out passion boldly, he returned, with his own glances, the most ineffable promises.

here have been many things written and said about that curious affair at the Sclatersbys, but
the entire history of it—well, there are reasons why you will never be able to trace it. Orson
ne is perhaps the only one who might tell some of the details; and he, as you will find
·sently, has utterly forgotten that night.

Time we went home, girls," said Vane, at last, disengaging himself gently from a number of
rm hands, and putting away, as he moved into freedom, more than one beautiful pair of
ıulders. He needed the fresh air; he was really quite worn out. But he still had a madcap notion
t in him; he still had a trump to play.

A pair of hose," he called out, "a pair of hose, with diamond-studded garters, to the one who
ll play 'follow' to my 'leader!'"

ınd the end of that dare-devil scamper did not come until the whole throng reached Madison
uare.

/ane plunged to the knees in the fountain.

hat chilled the chase. But one would not be denied. Hers was a dark type of beauty that
ded magnolias and the moon and the South to frame it properly. She lifted her skirts with a
le tinkling laugh, and ran to where Orson stood, splashing her way bravely through the water.
/ane looked at her and took her hand.

"I envy the prize I offered," he said to her.

CHAPTER VII.

Dawn found Orson Vane nodding in a hansom. He had told the man to drive to Claremont. The Palisades were just getting the first rosy streaks the sun was putting forth. The Hudson still lay with a light mist on it. The ascent to Claremont, in sunshine so clustered with beauty, was now deserted. A few carts belonging to the city were dragging along sleepily. Harlem was at the hour when the dregs of one day still taint the morn of the next one.

Vane was drowsy. He felt the need of a fillip. He did not like to think of getting back to his rooms and taking a nap. It was still too early, it seemed, for anything to eat or drink. He spied the Fort Lee ferry, and with it a notion came to him. The cabman was willing. In a few minutes he was aboard the ferry, and the cooler air that sweeps the Hudson was laving him. On the Jersey side he found a sleepy innkeeper who patched up a breakfast for him. He had, fortunately, some smokable cigars in his clothes. The day was well on when he reached the New York side of the river again, and gave "The Park!" as the cabman's orders.

His body now restored to energy again, his mind recounted the successes of the night. He really had nothing much to wish for. The men envied him to the point of hatred; the women adored him. He was the pet of the smartest people. He was shrewd enough, too, to be petted for a consideration; his adroitness in sales of Red Ribbon added comfortably to his income. He took pride in this, as if there had ever been a time, for several generations, when the name of Vane had not stood good for a million or so.

The Park was not well tenanted. Some robust members of the smart set were cantering about the bridle paths, and now and then a carriage turned a corner; but the people who preferred the Park for its own sake to the Park of the afternoon drive were, evidently, but few. Vane felt quite neglected; he was still able to count the number of times that he had bowed to familiars. The deserted state of the Park somewhat discounted the tonic effects of its morning freshness. Nature was nothing unless it was a background for man. The country was a place from which you could come to town. Still—there was really nothing better to do, this fine morning. He rather dreaded the thought of his rooms after the brilliance of the night.

His meditations ceased at approach of a girlish figure on horseback, a groom at a discreet distance behind.

It was Miss Vanlief.

He saw that she saw him, yet he saw no welcome in her eyes. He rapped for the hansom to stop; got out, and waved his hat elaborately at the young woman. She, in sheer politeness, had reined in her horse.

"A sweet day," he minced, "and jolly luck my meeting you! Thought it was rather dull in the Park, till you turned up. Sweet animal you're on." He looked up with that air that, the night before, had been so bewitching. Somehow, as the girl eyed him, he felt haggard. She was not smiling, not the least little bit.

"I have read about the affair at Mrs. Sclatersby's," she said.

"Really? Dreadful hurry these newspapers are always in, to be sure. It was really a great lark."

"It must have been," was her icy retort. She beckoned to the groom. "That—that sheet," she ordered, sharply, holding out one gauntleted hand. The groom gave her the folded newspaper. She began to read from it, in a bitter monotone:

"The antics of Mr. Orson Vane," she read, "for some time the subject of comment in society, have now reached the point where they deserve the censure of publicity. His doings at a certain fashionable dinner of last night were the subject of outspoken disgust at the prominent clubs later. Now that the case is openly discussed, it may be repeated that a prominent publication recently had occasion to refuse print to a distinctly questionable photograph of this young man, submitted, it is alleged, by himself. In the more staid social circles, one wonders how much longer Mrs. Carlos and the other leaders of the smartest set will continue to countenance such behavior."

Vane, as she read, was enjoying every inch of her. What freshness, what grace! What a Lady Godiva she would have made!

"Sweet of you to take such interest," he observed, as she handed the paper to the groom. "Malice, you know, sheer malice. Dare say I forgot to give that paper some news that I gave the others; they take that sort of thing so bitterly, you know. As for the photo—it was really awfully cunning. I'll send you one. Oh, must you go? I'm so cut up! Charming chat we've had, I'm sure."

She had given her horse a cut with the whip, had sent Vane a stare of the most open contempt, and was now off and away. Vane stood staring after her. "Very nice little filly," he murmured. "Very!"

Then he gave his house number to the cabman.

Turning into Park avenue, at Thirty-Ninth street, the horse slipped on the asphalt. The hansom spun on one wheel, and then crashed against a lamp-post. Vane was almost stunned, though there was no mark on him anywhere. He felt himself all over, but he could feel not as much as a lump. But his head ached horribly; he felt queerly incapable of thought. Whatever it was that had happened to him, it had stunned something in him. What that something was he did not realize even as he told Nevins, who opened the door to him in some alarm:

"Send the cab over to Mr. Reginald Hart's. Say I must—do you hear, Nevins?—I must have him here within the hour—if he has to come in a chair!"

Not even when he let the veil glide from the new mirror did he understand what part of him was stunned. He moved about in a sort of half wakefulness. The time he spent before Hart's arrival was all a stupor, spent on a couch, with eyes closed.

Hart came in feebly, leaning on a stick.

"Funny thing of you to do," he piped, "sending for me like this. What the—" He straightened himself in front of the new mirror, and, for an instant, swayed limply there. Then his stick took an upward swing, and he minced across the room vigorously. "Why, Vane," he said, "not ill, are you? Jove, you know, I've had a siege, myself. Feel nice and fit this minute, though. Shouldn't wonder if the effort to get here had done me good. What was the thing you wanted me for?"

Vane shook his head, feebly. "Upon my word, Hart, I don't know. I had an accident; cab crushed me; I was a little off my head, I think. All a mistake."

Sorry, I'm sure," lisped Hart, "hope it won't be anything real. I tell you I feel quite out of
ngs. All the other way with you, eh! Hear you're no end of a choice thing with the cafe au lait
1g. Well, adios!"

/ane lay quite still after the other had gone. When he spoke, it was to say, to the emptiness of
: room, but nodding to where Hart had last stood:

What a worm! What an utter worm!"

he voice was once more the voice of Orson Vane.

\s realization of that came to him, he spoke again, so loud that Nevins, without, heard it.

Thank God," he said.

CHAPTER VIII.

The time that had passed since he began the experiment with the Professor's mirror now filled Vane with horror. The life that had seemed so splendid, so triumphant to him a short while ago, now presented itself to him as despicable, mean, hateful. Now that he had safely ousted the soul of Reginald Hart he loathed the things that, under the dominance of that soul, he had done. The quick feeling of success that he had expected from his adventure into the realm of the mind was not his at all; his emotions were mixed, and in that mixture hatred of himself was uppermost. It was true: he had succeeded. The thoughts, the deeds of another man had become his thoughts, his deeds. The entire point of view had been, for the time, changed. But, where he had expected to keep the outland spirit in subjection, it was the reverse that had happened; the usurping soul had been in positive dominance; he had been carried along relentlessly by the desires and the reflections of that other.

The fact that he knew, now, to the very letter, the mind that animated that fellow, Reginald Hart, was small consolation to him. The odium of that reputation was inescapably his, Orson Vane's. Oh, the things he had said,—and thought,—and done! He had not expected that any man's mind could be so horrible as that. He thought of the visitation he had conjured upon himself, and so thinking, shuddered. How was he ever to elude the contempt that his masquerade, if he could call it so, would bring him?

Above all, that scene with Miss Vanlief came back to him with a bitter pang. What did it profit him, now, to fathom the foul depths of Reginald Hart's mind concerning any ever so girlish creature? It was he, Orson Vane, for all that it was possible to explain to the contrary, who had phrased Miss Vanlief's beauty in such abominable terms.

Consternation sat on his face like a cloud. He could think of no way out of the dark alley into which he had put himself.

Each public appearance of his now had its tortures. Men who had respected him now avoided him; women to whom he had once condescended were now on an aggravating plane of intimacy. Sometimes he could almost feel himself being pointed out on the street.

The mental and physical reaction was beginning to trace itself on his face. He feared his Florentine mirrors now almost as much as the Professor's. The blithe poise had left him. He brooded a good deal. His insight into another nature than his own filled him with a sense of distaste for the human trend toward evil.

He spent some weeks away from town, merely to pick up his health again. His strength returned a little, but the joy of life came back but tardily.

On his first day in town he met Moncreith. There was an ominous wrinkle gathering in the other's forehead, but Vane braved all chance of a rebuff.

"Luke," he said, "don't you know I've been ill? You can't think how ill I've been. Do you remember I told you I was going abroad? I've been abroad, mentally; I have, Luke, really I have. It's like a bad dream to me. You know what I mean."

Moncreith found his friend rather pathetic. At their last meeting he had been hot in jealousy of

son. Now he could afford to pity him. He had made Jeannette Vanlief's acquaintance, and he
od quite well with her. He had made up his mind to stand yet better; he was, in fact, in love
th her. He was quite sure that Vane had quite put himself out of that race. So he took the
er's hand, and walked amicably to the Town and Country Club with him.

You have been doing strange things," he ventured.

Strange," echoed Vane, "strange isn't the word! Ghastly, horrible—awful things I've been
ng. I wish I could explain. But it—it isn't my secret, Luke. All I can say is: I was ill. I am, I
pe, quite well again."

t seemed an age since he had spent an hour or so in his favorite club. The air of the members
s unmistakably frosty. The conversation shrank audibly. He was glad when Moncreith found a
luded corner and bore him to it. But he was not a bright companion; his own thoughts were
depressing to allow of his presenting a sparkling surface to the world. They talked in mere
tches, in curt syllables.

I've seen a good deal of Miss Vanlief," said Moncreith, with conscious triumph.

Oh," said Vane, with a start, "Miss Vanlief? So you know her? Is she—is she well?"

Quite. I see her almost every day."

Fortunate man!" sighed Vane. He was a little weary of life. He wanted to tell somebody what
dreams about Miss Vanlief were; he wanted to cry out loud, "She is the dearest, sweetest girl
he world!" merely to efface, in his own mind, the alien thought of her that had come to him
eks ago. Moncreith did not seem the one to utter this cry to. Moncreith was too engrossed in
own success. He could bear Moncreith's company no longer, not just then. He muttered lame
rds; he stumbled out to the avenue.

ome echo of an instinct turned his steps to the little bookshop.

t was quite empty of customers. He passed his fingers over the back of books that he thought
ss Vanlief might have handled. It was an absurd whim, a childish trick. Yet it soothed him
ceptibly. Our nerves control our bodies and our nerves are slaves of our imaginations.

le was turning to go, when his eye fell on a parcel lying on the counter. It was addressed to
liss Jeannette Vanlief."

Jeannette, Jeannette!" he said the name over to himself time and again. It brought the image of
before him more plainly than ever. The sunset glint in her hair, the roses and lilies of her
n, the melody in her voice! The charm with which she had first met him, in that very shop. It
came to him keenly. The more remote the possibility of his gaining her seemed, the more he
ged the thought of her. He admitted to himself now, all the more since his excursion into an
ominable side of human nature, that she was the most unspoilt creature in his world. A girl
th that face, that hair, that wit, was sure to be of a charm that could never lose its flavor; the
urement of her was a thing that could never die.

Nothing but thoughts of this girl came to him on the way to his rooms. Once in his own place,
felt that his reflections on Miss Vanlief had served him as a tonic. He felt an energy once
re, a vigor, a desire for action. In that mood he turned fiercely upon some of the drawings on
walls. He called Nevins, and had a heap made of the things that now filled him with loathing.

"All of the Beardsleys must come down," he ordered. "No; not all. The portrait of Mantegna may stay. That has nobility; the others have the genius of hidden evil. They take too much of the trapping from our horrible human nature. The funeral procession by Willette may hang; his Montmartre things are trivially indecent. Heine and his grotesqueries may stay in jail for all I care. Leave one or two of Thoeny's blue dragoons. Leandre's crowned heads will do me no harm; I can see past their cruelties. But take the Gibsons away; they are relegated to the matinee girl. What is to be done with them? Really, Nevins, don't worry me about such things. Sell them, give them, lose them: I don't care. There's only one man in the world who'd really adore them, and he—" he clenched his hands as he thought of Hart,—"he is a worm, a worm that dieth and yet corrupts everything about him."

He sat down, when this clearance was over, and wrote a rather long letter to Professor Vanlief. He told as much as he could bring himself to tell of the result of the experiment. He begged the Professor, knowing the circumstances as no other did, to do what was possible to reinstate him, Vane, in the esteem of Miss Vanlief. As to whether he meant to go on with further experiments; he had not yet made up his mind. There were consequences, obligations, following on this clear reading of other men's souls, that he had not counted upon.

CHAPTER IX.

To cotton-batting and similar unromantic staples the great house of R.S. Neargood & Co. first owed the prosperity that later developed into world-wide fame. It was success in cotton-batting that enabled the firm to make those speculations that eventually placed millions to its credit, and familiarized the Bourse and Threadneedle Street with its name.

What ever else can be said of cotton-batting, however, it is hardly a topic of smart conversation. So in smart circles there was never any mention of cotton-batting when the name Neargood came up. Instead, it was customary to refer to them as "the people, you know, who built the Equator Palace for the Tropical Government, and all that sort of thing." A certain vagueness is indispensable to polite talk.

Yet not even this detail of politics and finance counted most in the smart world. The name of Neargood might never have been heard of in that world if it had not been for the beautiful daughters of the house of Neargood. There is nothing, nowadays, like having handsome daughters. You may have made your millions in pig, or your thousands in whisky, but, in the eyes of the complaisant present, the curse dies with the debut of a beautiful daughter. It is true that the smart sometimes make an absurd distinction between the older generation and the new; sometimes a barrier is raised for the daughter that checks the mother; but caprice was ever one of the qualities of smartness.

Through two seasons the beautiful Misses Neargood—Mary and Alice—reigned as belles. They were both good to look at, tall, stately, with distinct profiles. There was not much to choose, so to put it, between them. Mary was the handsomer; Alice the cleverer. Through two seasons the society reporters, on the newspapers that are yellow as well as those that make one blue, exhausted the well of journalese in chronicling the doings of these two young women. The climax of descriptive eloquence was reached on the occasion of the double wedding of Mary and Alice Neargood.

Mary changed the name of Neargood for that of Spalding-Wentworth; Alice became Mrs. Van Fenno.

Up to this time—as far, at least, as was observable—these two sisters had dwelt together in amity. Never had the spirits of envy or uncharitableness entered them. But after marriage there came to each of them that stormy petrel of Unhappiness, Ambition.

As a composer of several songs and light operas, Van Fenno was fairly well known. Spalding-Wentworth was known as a man of Western wealth, of Western blue blood, and of prominence in the smart set. For some time the worldly successes of the Van Fennos did not disturb Mrs. Spalding-Wentworth at all. Her husband was smart, since he moved with the smart; he and his cousin were the leaders in a great many famous ways, notably in fashion and in golf. From the smart point of view the Van Fennos were not in the hunt with the other family.

Mrs. Van Fenno chafed and churned a little in silence, but hope did not die in her. She made up her mind to be as prominent as her sister or perish in the attempt.

She did not have to perish. Things took a turn, as they will even in the smart world, and there came a time when it was fashionable to be intellectual. The smart set turned from the distractions of dinners and divorces to the allurements of the arts. Music, painting and literature became the idols of the hour. With that bland, heedless facility that distinguishes To-day, the men and women of fashion became quickly versed in the patter of the Muses.

The Van Fennos became the rage. Everybody talked of his music and her charm. Where the reporters had once used space in describing Spalding-Wentworth's leadership in a cotillon or conduct of a coach, they were now required to spill ink in enumeration of "those present" at Mrs. Van Fenno's "musical afternoons."

Wherefore there was a cloud on the fair brow of Mary Wentworth. Her intimates were privileged to call her that. Ordinary mortals, omitting the hyphen, would have been frozen with a look.

When there is a cloud on the wife's brow it bodes ill for the husband. The follies of a married man should be dealt with leniently; they are mostly of his wife's inspiration. One day the cloud cleared from Mary Wentworth's brow. She was sitting at breakfast with her husband.

"Why, Clarence," she exclaimed, with a suddenness that made him drop his toast, "there's literature!"

"Where?" said Clarence, anxiously. "Where?" He looked about, eager to please.

"Stupid," said his wife. "I mean—why shouldn't we, that is, you—" She looked at him, sure that he would understand without her putting the thing into syllables. "Yes," she repeated, "literature is the thing. There it is, as easy, as easy—"

"Hasn't it always been there?" asked her dear, dense husband. A woman may brood over a thing, you see, for months, and the man will not get so much as a suspicion.

She went on as if he had never spoken. "Literature is the easiest. Clarence, you must write novels!"

He buttered himself another slice of toast.

"Certainly, my dear," he nodded, with a pleasant smile. "Quite as you please."

It was in this way that the Spalding-Wentworth novels were incited. The art of writing badly is, unfortunately, very easy. In painting and in music some knowledge of technic is absolutely necessary, but in literature the art of writing counts last, and technic is rarely applauded. The fact remains that the smart set thought the Spalding-Wentworth novels were "so clever!" Mrs. Van Fenno was utterly crushed. Mary Wentworth informed an eager world that her husband's next novel would be illustrated with caricatures by herself; she had developed quite a trick in that direction. Now and again her husband refused to bother his head with ambitions, and devoted himself entirely to red coats and white balls. Mrs. Wentworth's only device at such times was to take desperately to golf herself. She really played well; if she had only had staying power, courage, she might have gone far. But, if she could not win cups, she could look very charming on the clubhouse lawn. One really does not expect more from even a queen.

It did not disturb Mrs. Wentworth at all to know that, where he was best known, her husband's artistic efforts were considered merely a joke. She knew that everyone had some mask or other to hold up to the world; and she knew there was nothing to fear from a brute of a man or two. In her art she agreed with them; she knew her husband was a large, kindly, clumsy creature; a useful, werful person, who needed guidance.

Kindly and clumsy—Clarence Spalding-Wentworth had title to those two adjectives: there was denying that. It was his kindliness that moved him, after a busy day at a metropolitan golf irnament, toward Orson Vane's house. He had heard stories of Vane's illness; they had been at lege together; he wanted to see him, to have a chat, a smoke, a good, chummy hour or two.

t was his clumsiness that brought about the incident that came to have such memorable isequences. Nevins told him Mr. Vane was out; Wentworth thought he would go in and have a k at Vane's rooms, anyway; sit down, perhaps, and write him a note. Nevins had swung the tain to behind him when Wentworth's heel caught in the wrapping around the new mirror. Ie looked into the pool of glass blankly.

Funny thing to cover up a mirror like that!" he told himself. He flung the stuff over the frame elessly. It merely hung by a thread. Almost any passing wind would be sure to lift it off. Wonder where he keeps his smokes?" he hummed to himself, striding up and down, like a od natured mammoth.

Ie found some cigars began puffing at one with an audible satisfaction, and at last let himself wn to an ebony escritoire that he could have smashed with one hand. He wrote a scrawl; ited again, whistled, looked out of the window, picked up a book, peered at the pictures, and n, with a puff of regret, strode out.

As he passed the Professor's mirror the current of air he made swept the curtain from the glass d left it exposed.

CHAPTER X.

At about the time that Wentworth was scrawling his note in Vane's rooms a slender young woman, dressed in a grey that shimmered like the winter-sea in sunlight, wearing a hat that had the air of having lit upon her hair for the moment only,—merely to give the world an instant's glance at the gracious combination that woman's beauty and man's millinery could effect—was coming out from one of those huge bazaars where you can buy almost everything in the world except the things you want. As she reached the doors, a young man, entering, brushed her arm; his sleeve caught her portemonnaie. He stooped for it, offered it hastily, and then—and not until then, gave a little "Oh!" of—what was it, joy? or mere wonder, or both?

"Oh," he repeated, "I can't go in—now. It's—it's ages since I could say two words to you. 'Good-morning!' and 'How do you do?' has been the limit of our talk. Besides, you have a parcel. It weighs, at the very least, an ounce. I could never think of letting you tire yourself so." He took the flimsy mite from her, and ranged his steps to hers.

It was true, what he had said about their brief encounters. Do what she would to forget that morning in the Park, and the weeks before it, Jeannette Vanlief had not quite succeeded. Not even the calm dissertations of her father, the arguments pointing to the unfathomable freakishness of human nature, had altogether ousted her aversion to Orson Vane. It was an aversion made the more keen because it came on the heels of a strong liking. She had been prepared to like this young man. Something about him had drawn her; and then had come the something that had simply flung her away. Yet, to-day, he seemed to be the Orson Vane that she had been prepared to like.

She remembered some of the strange things her father had been talking about. She noted, as Orson spoke, that the false tenor note was gone out of his voice. But she was still a little fluttered; she could not quite trust herself, or him.

"But I am only going to the car," she declared. "It will hardly be worth while. I mustn't take you out of your way."

"I see," he regretted, "you've not forgotten. I can't explain; I was—I think I was a little mad. Perhaps it is in the family. But—I wish you would imagine, for to-day, that we had only just known each other a very little while, that we had been in that little bookshop only a day or so ago, that you had read the book, and we had met again, and—." He was looking at her with a glow in his eyes, a tenderness—! Her eyes met his for only an instant, but they fathomed, in that instant, that there was only homage, and worship, and—and something that she dared not spell, even to her soul—in them. That burning greed that she had seen in the Park was not there.

She smiled, wistfully, hesitatingly. Yet it was enough for him to cling to; it buoyed his mood to higher courage.

"Let us pretend," he went on, "that there are no streetcars in the town. Let us be primitive; let us play we are going to take a peep-show from the top of the Avenue stage! Oh—please! It gets you just as near, you know; and if you like we can go on, and on, and do it all over again. Think of the tops of the hats and bonnets one sees from the roof! It's such a delightful picture of the

enue; you see all the little marionettes going like beads along the string. And then, think of the
nger of the climb to the roof! It is like the Alps. You never know, until you are there, whether
u will arrive in one piece or in several. Come," he laughed, for she was now really smiling,
enly, sweetly, "let us be good children, come in from Westchester County, to see the big city."
Perhaps," she ventured, "we will make it the fashion. And that would spoil it for so many of
plainer people."
Oh," and he waved his hand, "after us—the daily papers! Let us pretend—I beg your pardon,
me pretend—youth, and high spirits, and the intention to enjoy to-day."
A rattling and a scraping on the asphalt warned them of an approaching stage, and after a
amble, that had its shy pleasures for both, they found themselves on the top of the old relic.
It is a bit of the Middle Ages," said Orson, "look at those horses! Aren't they delightfully
nder? And the paint! Do you notice the paint? And the stories those plush seats down below
could tell! Think of the misers and the millionaires, the dowagers and the drabs, that have let
se old stages bump them over Murray Hill! You can't have that feeling about a street-car, not
e of the electric ones, at any rate. Do you know the story of the New Yorker who was trying to
ep in a first-class compartment on a French railway? There was a collision, and he was
ched ten feet onto a coal-heap. He said he thought he was at home and he was getting off the
ge at Forty-Second street."
They were passing through the most frequented part of the avenue. Noted singers and famous
yers passed them; old beaux and fresh belles; political notabilities and kings of corruption. A
ious leader of cotillions, a beauty whose profile vied with her Boston terriers for being her
ef distinction, and a noted polo-player came upon the scene and vanished again. Vane and his
npanion gave, from time to time, little nods to right and left. Their friends stared at them a
le, but that caused them no sorrow. Automobiles rushed by. They looked down upon them,
ty in their ruined tower.
As a show," said Vane, "it is admirably arranged. It moves with a beautiful precision. There is
hing hurried about it; the illusion of life is nearly complete. Some of them, I suppose, really
alive?"
I am not sure," she answered, gravely. "Sometimes I think they merely move because there is
utton being pressed somewhere; a button we cannot see, and that they spend their lives hiding
m us."
I dare say you are right. In the words of Fay Templeton, 'I've been there and I know.' I have
de my little detours: but the lane had, thank fortune, a turning."
he saw through his playfulness, and her eyes went up to his in a sympathy—oh, it made him
l for sweetness.
I am glad," she said, simply.
But we are getting serious again," he remonstrated, "that would never do. Have we not sworn
be children? Let us pretend—let us pretend!" He looked at the grey roofs, the spires oozing
m the hill to the sky. He looked at the grey dream beside him: so grey, so fair, so crowned
th the hue of the sun before the world had made him so brazen. "Let us pretend," he went on,

after a sigh, "that we are bound for the open road, and that we are to come to an inn, and that we will order something to eat. We—"

"Oh," she laughed, "you men, you men! Always something to eat!"

"You see, we are of coarse stuff; we cannot sup on star-dust, and dine on bubbles. But—this is only to pretend! An imaginary meal is sometimes so much more fun than a real one. At a real one, you see, I would have to try to eat, and I could not spend the whole time looking at you, and watching the sunshine on your hair, and the lilies—" He caught his breath sharply, with a little clicking noise. "Dear God," he whispered, "the lilies again! And I had never seen them until now."

"You are going to be absurd," she said, though her voice was hardly a rebuke.

"And wouldn't I have excuse," he asked, "for all the absurdities in the world! I want to be as absurd as I can; I want to think that there's nothing in the world any uglier than—you."

"And will you dine off that thought?"

"Oh, no; that is merely one of the condiments. I keep that in reach, while the other things come and go. I tell you: how would it be if we began with a bisque of crab? The tenderest pink, you know, and not the ghost of any spice that you can distinguish; a beautiful, creamy blend."

"You make it sound delicious," she admitted.

"We take it slowly, you know, religiously. The conversation is mostly with the eyes. Dinner conversation is so often just as vapid as dinner-music! The only point in favor of dinner-music is that we are usually spared the sight of it. There is no truth more abused than the one that music must be heard and not seen. When I am king I mean to forbid any singing or playing of instruments within sight of the public; it spoils all the pleasure of the music when one sees the uglinesses in its execution."

"But people would not thank you if you kept the sight of Paderewski or De Pachmann from them."

"They might not thank me at first, but they would learn gratitude in the end, A contortionist is quite as oppressive a sight as an automaton. No; I repeat, performers of music should never, never be visible. It is a blow in the face of the art of music; it puts it on the plane of the theatre. What persons of culture want to do is to listen, to listen, to listen; to shut the eyes, and weave fancies about the strains as they come from an unseen corner. Is there not always a subtle charm about music floating over a distance? That is a case in point; that same charm should always be preserved. The pianist, the soloist of any sort, as well as the orchestra, or the band—except in the case of the regimental band, in battle or in review, where actual spectacle, and visible encouragement are the intention—should never be seen. There should always be a screen, a curtain, between us and the players. It would make the trick of music criticism harder, but it would still leave us the real judges. Take out of music criticism the part that covers fingering, throat manipulation, pedaling, and the like, and what have you left? These fellows judge what they see more than what they hear. To give a proper judgment of the music that comes from the unseen; that is the only test of criticism. There can be no tricks, no paddings."

"But the opera?" wondered the girl.

The opera? Oh, the opera is, at best, a contradiction in terms. But I do not waive my theory for
 sake of opera. It should be seen as little as any other form of music. The audience, supplied
th the story of the dramatic action, should follow the incidents by ear, not by eye. That would
the true test of dramatic writing in music. We would, moreover, be spared the absurdity of
tching singers with beautiful voices make themselves ridiculous by clumsy actions. As to
nic opera—the music's appeal would suffer no tarnish from the merely physical fascination of
 star or the chorus ... I know the thought is radical; it seems impossible to imagine a piano
ital without long hair, electric fingers, or visible melancholia; opera with only the box-holders
appeals to the eye seems too good to be true; but—I assure you it would emancipate music
m all that now makes it the most vicious of the arts. Painters do not expect us to watch them
nting, nor does the average breed of authors—I except the Manx—like to be seen writing. Yet
 musician—take away the visible part of his art, and he is shorn of his self-esteem. I assure
u I admire actors much more than musicians; actors are frankly exponents of nothing that
quires genius, while musicians pretend to have an art that is over and above the art of the
mposer.... Music—"
Do you realize," interrupted the girl, with a laugh that was melody itself, "that you are feasting
 upon dinner-music without dinner. It must be ages since we began that imaginary feast. But
w, I am quite sure we are at the black coffee. And I have been able to notice nothing except
ur ardor in debate. You were as eager as if you were being contradicted."
You see," he said, "it only proves my point. Dinner-music is an abomination. It takes the taste
the food away. While I was playing, you admit, you tasted nothing between the soup and the
ffee. Whereas, in point of fact—"
Or fancy?"
As you please. At any rate—the menu was really something out of the common. There were
ne delightful wines. A sherry that the innkeeper had bought of a bankrupt nobleman; so would
 his fable for the occasion, and we would believe it, because, in cases of that sort, it takes a
y bad wine to make one pooh-pooh its pedigree. A Madeira that had been hidden in a cellar
ce 1812. We would believe that, every word of it, because we would know that there was
lly no Madeira in all the world; and we must choose between insulting our stomachs or our
elligence. And then the coffee. It would come in the tiniest, most transparent, most fragile—"
Yes," she laughed, "I dare say. As transparent and as fragile as the entire fabric of our repast, I
ve no doubt. But—pity me, do!—I shall have to leave the beautiful banquet about where you
ve put it, in the air. I have a ticking conscience here that says—"
Oh, hide it," he supplicated, "hide it. Watches are nothing but mechanisms that are jealous of
ppiness; whenever there is a happy hour a watch tries to end it. When I am king I shall prohibit
 manufacture and sale of watches. The fact that they may be carried about so easily is one of
ir chief vices; one never knows nowadays from what corner a woman will not bring one; they
ry them on their wrists, their parasols, their waists, their shoulders. Can you be so cruel as to
that little golden monster spoil me my hour of happiness—"
But I would have to be cruel one way or the other. You see, my father will wonder what has

become of me. He expects me to dinner."

"Ah, well," he admitted soberly, if a little sadly, "we must not keep him waiting. You must tell the Professor where we have been, and what we said, and how silly I was, and—Heigho, I wish I could tell you how the little hour with you has buoyed me up. Your presence seems to stir my possibilities for good. I wish I could see you oftener. I feel like the provincial who says good-bye with a: 'May I come 'round this evening?' as a rider."

"A doubtful compliment, if I make you rustic," she said. "But I have something on this evening; an appointment with a man. The most beautiful man in the world, and the best, and the kindest—"

"His name?" he cried, with elaborate pretense of melodrama, for he saw that she was full of whimsies.

"Professor Vanlief," she curtsied.

They were walking, by now, in the shade of the afternoon sun. Vane saw a stage approaching them, one that would take him back to the lower town. She saw it, too, and his intention. She shook hands with him, and took time to say, softly:

"Do you never ride in the Park any more?"

"Oh," he said, "tell me when. To-morrow morning? At McGowan's Pass? At ten? Oh, how I wish that stage was not coming so fast!"

In their confusion, and their joyous sense of having the same absurd thought in common, they both laughed at the notion of a Fifth avenue stage ever being too fast. Yet this one, and Time, sped so swiftly that Vane could only shake hands hastily with his fair companion, look at her worshipfully, and jump upon the clattering vehicle.

He would never have believed that so ramshackle a conveyance could have harbored so many dreams as had been his that day.

That thought was his companion all the way home. That, and efforts to define his feelings toward Miss Vanlief. Was it love? What else could it be! And if it was, was he ready, for her, to give up those ambitions of still further sounding hitherto unexplored avenues of the human mind? Was this fragile bit of grace and glamour to come between him and the chance of opening a new field to science? Had he not the opportunity to become famous, or, at the very least, to become omnipotent in reading the hearts, the souls, of men? Were not the possibilities of the Professor's discovery unlimited? Was it not easy by means of that mirror in his rooms, for any chief of police in the world to read the guilt or innocence of every accused man? Yet, on the other hand, would marriage interfere? Yes; it would. One could not serve two such goddesses as woman and science. He would have to make up his mind, to decide.

But, in the meanwhile, there was plenty of time. Surely, for the present, he could be happy in the thought of the morrow, of the ride they were to take in the Park, of the cantering, the chattering together, the chance to see the morning wind spin the twists of gold about her cheeks and bring the sparkle to her eyes.

He let himself into his house without disturbing any of the servants. He passed into his room. He lifted the curtain of the doorway with one hand, and with the other turned the button that lighted the room. As the globes filled with light they showed him his image in the new mirror.

He reeled against the wall with the surprise of the thing. He noted the mirror's curtain in a heap at the foot of the frame. Perhaps, after all, it had been merely the wind.

He summoned Nevins. The curtain he replaced on the staring face of the mirror. Whence the thought came from, he did not know, but it occurred to him that the scene was like a scene from a novel.

"Nevins," he asked, "was anyone in my rooms?"

"Mr. Spalding-Wentworth, sir."

Orson Vane laughed,—a loud, gusty, trumpeting laugh.

He understood. But he understood, also, that the accident that had brought the soul of Spalding-Wentworth into his keeping had decreed, also, that the dominance should not be, as on a former time, with the usurper.

He knew that the soul of Spalding-Wentworth, to which he gave the refuge of his own body, was a small soul.

Yet even little souls have their spheres of influence.

CHAPTER XI.

It was a morning such as the wild flowers, out in the suburban meadows, must have thought fit for a birthday party. As for the town, it lost, under that keen air and gentle sun, whatever of garish and unhealthy glamour it had displayed the night before.

"The morning," Orson Vane had once declared, in a moment of revelation, "is God's, and the night is man's." He was speaking, of course, of the town. In the severe selectiveness that had grown upon him after much rout and riot through other lands, he pretended that the town was the only spot on the map. Certainly this particular morning seemed to bear out something of this saying; it swept away the smoke and the taint, the fever and the flush of the night before; the visions of limelights and glittering crystals and enmillioned vice fled before the gust of ozone that came pouring into the streets. Before night, to be sure, man would have asserted himself once more; the pomp and pageant of the primrose path would have ousted, with its artificial charm, the clean, sweet freshness of the morning.

The grim houses on upper Fifth avenue put on semblance of life reluctantly that morning. Houses take on the air of their inmates; these houses wore their best manner only under artificial lights. Surly grooms and housemaids went muttering and stumbling about the areas. Sad-faced wheelmen flashed over the asphalt, cursing the sprinkling carts. It was not too early for the time-honored preoccupation of the butcher cart, which consists of turning corners as if the world's end was coming. Pallid clubmen strode furtively in the growing sunshine. To them, as to the whole town, the sun and its friend, the breeze, came as a tonic and a cure.

So strange a thing is the soul of man that Orson Vane, riding towards the Park that morning, caught only vague, fleeting impressions of the actual beauty of the day. He simply wondered, every foot of the way to McGowan's Pass, whether Miss Vanlief played golf. The first thing he said to her after they had exchanged greetings, was:

"Of course you golf?"

She looked at him in alarm. There was something—something, but what was it?—in his voice, in his eye. She had expected a reference to the day before, to their infantile escapade on the roof of the coach. Instead, this banale, this stupid, this stereotyped phrase! Her flowerlike face clouded; she gave her mare the whip.

"No," she called out, "I cannot bear the game." His horse caught the pace with difficulty; the groom was left far out of sight, beyond a corner. But the diversion had not touched Vane's trend of thought at all.

"Oh," he assured her, when the horses were at an amble again, "it's one of those things one has to do. Some things have to be done, you know; society won't stand for anything less, you know, oh, no. I have to play golf, you know; part of my reputation."

"I didn't know," she faltered. She tried to remember when Orson Vane had ever been seen on either the expert or the duffer list at the golf matches.

"Oh, yes; people expect it of me. If I don't play I have to arrange tournaments. Handicapping is great fun; ever try it? No? You should. Makes one feel quite like a judge at sessions. Oh, there's nothing like golf. Not this year, at least. Next year it may be something else. I may have to take to polo or tennis. One is expected to show the way, you know; a man in my position—" He looked at her with a kind of 'bland, blunt, clumsy egoism, that made her wonder where was the Orson Vane of yesterday. This riddle began to sadden her. Perhaps it was true, as she had heard somewhere, that the man was mentally unbalanced; that he had his—well, his bad days. She sighed. She had looked forward to this ride in the Park; she admitted that to herself. Not in a whole afternoon spent with Luke Moncreith had she felt such happy childishness stirring in her as yesterday, in the hour with Orson Vane. And now—She sighed.

The hum of an approaching automobile reached them, the glittering vehicle proclaiming its progress in that purring stage whisper that is still the inalienable right of even the newest "bubble" machine. The coat worn by the smart young person on the seat would have shocked the unenlightened, for that sparkling, tingling morning it struck the exact harmonious note of artifice.

Orson Vane bowed. It was "the" Miss Carlos. Just as there is only one Mrs. Carlos, so there is only one Miss Carlos.

"She plays a decent game," said Vane to his companion.

"Of life?"

"No; golf." He looked at her in amazement. Life! What was life compared to golf? Life? For most people it was, at best, a foozle. Nearly everybody pressed; very few followed through, and the bunkers—good Lord, the bunkers!

"I'm thinking of writing a golfing novel," began Orson, after an interval in which he managed to wonder whether one couldn't play golf from horseback.

"Oh," said Miss Vanlief wearily, "how does one set about it!"

He was quite unaware of her weariness. He chirped his answer with blind enthusiasm.

"It's very easy," he declared. "There are always a lot of women, you know, who are aching to do things in that line. You give them the prestige of your name, that's all. One of them writes the thing; you simply keep them from foozling the phrases now and then. Another illustrates it."

"And does anyone buy it?"

"Oh, all the smart people do. It's one of those things one is supposed to do. There's no particular reason or sense in it; but smart people expect one another to read things like that. The newspapers get quite silly over such books. Then, after novels, I think, I shall take to having them done over for the stage? Don't you think a golfing comedy, with a sprinkling of profanity and Scotch whiskey, would be all the rage?"

Jeannette Vanlief reined in her mare. She looked at Orson Vane; looked him, as much as she could, through and through. Was it all a stupid jest? She could find nothing but dense earnestness in her face, in his eyes. Oh, the riddle was too tiresome, too hopeless. It was simply not the same man at all! She gave it up, gave him up.

"Do you mind," she said, "if I ride home now? I'm tired."

It should have been a blow in the face, but Orson Vane never so much as noticed it.

"Tired?" he repeated. "Oh; all right. We'll turn about. Rather go back alone? Oh, all right. Wish you'd learn to play golf; you really must!" And upon that he let her canter away, the groom following, some little wonder on his impassive front.

As for Jeannette Vanlief she burst into her father's room a little later, and then into tears.

"And I wanted to love him!" she wailed presently, from out her confusion and her distress.

The Professor was patting her hair, and wondering what in all the world was the matter. At her speech, he thought he saw a light.

"And why not?" he asked, soothingly, "He seems quite estimable. He was here only a moment ago?"

"Who was here?" she asked in bewilderment.

"Mr. Moncreith."

At that she laughed. The storm was over, the sunshine peeped out again.

"You dear, blind comfort, you!" she said, "What do I care if a thousand Moncreiths—"

"Then it's Orson Vane," said the Professor, not so blind after all. "Well, dear, and what has he been doing now?"

He listened to her rather rambling, rather spasmodic recital; listened and grew moody, though he could scarce keep away some little mirth. He saw through these masquerades, of course. Who else, if not he? Poor Jeannette! So she had set her happy little heart upon that young man? A young man who, to serve both their ends, was playing chameleon. A young man who was mining greater secrets from the deeps of the human soul than had ever been mined before. A wonderful young man, but—would that make for Jeannette's happiness? At any rate he, the Professor, would have to keep an eye open for Vane's doings. There was no knowing what strange ways these borrowed souls might lead to. He wondered who it was that, this time, had been rifled of his soul.

Wonder did not long remain the adjuncts of the Professor and his daughter only. The whole world of society began to wonder, as time went on, at the new activities of Orson Vane. Wonder ceased, presently, and there was passive acceptance of him in his new role. Fashions, after all, are changed so often in the more external things, that the smart set would not take it as a surprising innovation if some people took to changing their souls to suit the social breeze.

Orson Vane took a definite place in the world of fashion that season. He became the arbiter of golf; he gave little putting contests for women and children; he looked after the putting greens of a number of smart clubs with as much care as a woman gives her favorite embroideries. He took to the study of the Turkish language. There were rumors that he meant to become the Minister to Turkey. He traveled a great deal, and he published a book called "The Land of the Fez." Another little brochure bearing his name was "The Caddy; His Ailments and Diseases." It was rumored that he was busy in dramatization of his novel, "Five Loaves and Two Fishes!" When Storman Pasha made his memorable visit to the States it was Orson Vane who became his guide and friend. A jovial club of newspaper roysterers poked fun at him by nominating him for Mayor. He went through it all with a bland humorlessness and stubborn dignity that nothing could affront. His indomitable energy, his intense seriousness about everything, kept smart society unalterably loyal. He led its cotillions, arranged its more sober functions, and was a household word with the outsiders that reach society only through the printed page. His novels—whether they were his own or done for him hardly matters—were just dull enough to offend nobody. The most indolent dweller in Vanity Fair could affect his books without the least mental exertion. The lives of our fashionables are too full, too replete with a multitude of interests and excitements, to allow of the concentration proper for the reading of scintillating dialogue, or brilliant observations. Orson Vane appeared to gauge his public admirably; he predominated in the outdoor life, in golf, in yachting, in coaching, yet he did not allow anyone else to dispute the region of the intellect, of indoors, with him. He shone, with a severe dimness, in both fields.

Jeannette Vanlief, meanwhile, lost much of the sparkle she had hitherto worn. She drooped perceptibly. The courtship of Luke Moncreith left her listless; he persevered on the strength of his own ambition rather than her encouragement. His daughter's looks at last began seriously to worry Professor Vanlief. Something ought to be done. But what? It was apparently Orson Vane's intention to keep that borrowed soul with him for a long time. In the meanwhile Jeannette.... The Professor, the more he considered the matter, felt the more strongly that just as he was the one who had given Vane this power, so had he the right, if need be, to interfere. The need was urgent. The masquerade must be put an end to.

His resolve finally taken, Professor Vanlief paid a visit to Orson Vane's house. Vane was, as he had hoped, not at home. He cross-questioned Nevins.

The man was only too willing to admit that his master's actions were queer. But Mr. Vane had given him warning to that effect; he must have felt it coming on. It was a malady, no doubt. For his part he thought it was something that Mr. Vane would wish to cure rather than endure. He didn't pretend to understand his master of late, but—

The Professor put a period to the man's volubility with some effort.

"I want you," he urged, "to jog your memory a little. Never mind the symptoms. Give me straightforward answers. Now—did you touch the new mirror, leaving it uncovered, at any time within the past few weeks?"

"Oh," was the answer, "the new mirror, is it! I knows well the uncanny thing was sure to make trouble for me. But I gives you my word, as I hopes to be saved, that I've never so much as brushed the dust off it, much less taken the curtain off. It's fearsome, is that mirror, I'm thinking. It's—"

"Then think back," pressed the Professor, again stemming the tide of the other's talk relentlessly, "think back: was anyone, ever, at any time, alone in Mr. Vane's rooms? Think, think!"

"I disremember," stammered Nevins. "I think not—Oh, wait! It was a long time ago, but I think a gentleman wrote Mr. Vane a note once, and I, having work in the other rooms, let him be undisturbed. But I told the master about it, the minute he came in, sir. He was not the least vexed, sir. Oh, I'm easy in my mind about that time."

"Yes, yes,—but the gentleman's name!" The Professor shook the man's shoulder quite roughly.

"His name? Oh, it was just Mr. Spalding-Wentworth, sir, that was all."

The Professor sat down with a laugh. Spalding-Wentworth! He laughed again.

Nevins had the air of one aggrieved. "Mr. Vane laughed, too, I remember, when I told him.

Just the minute I told him, sir, he laughed. I've puzzled over it, time and again, why—"

The Professor left Nevins puzzling. There was no time to be lost. He remembered now that Spalding-Wentworth had for some time been ailing. The world, in its devotion to Orson Vane, had forgotten, almost, that such a person as Spalding-Wentworth had ever existed. To be forgotten one has only to disappear. Dead men's shoes are filled nowhere so quickly as in Vanity Fair; though, to be paradoxic, for the most part they are high-heeled slippers.

It took some little time, some work, to arrange what the Professor had decided must be done. He went about his plans with care and skill. He suborned Nevins easily enough, using, chiefly, the plain truth. Nevins, with the superstition of his class, was willing to believe far greater mysteries than the Professor half hinted at. By Nevins' aid it happened that Orson Vane slept, one night, face to face with the polished surface of the new mirror. In the morning it was curtained as usual.

That morning Augustus Vanlief called at the Wentworth house. He asked for Mrs. Wentworth. He went to his point at once.

"You know who I am, I dare say, Mrs. Wentworth. You love your husband, I am sure; you will pardon my intrusion when I tell you that perhaps I can do something the best thing of all—for him. It is, in its way, a matter of life and death. Do the doctors give you any hope?"

Mrs. Wentworth, her beauty now tired and touched by traces of spoilt ambition, made a listless motion with her hands.

"I don't know why I should tell you," she said, "or why I should not. They tell me vague things, the doctors do, but I don't believe they know what is the matter."

"Do you?"

"I?" she looked at Vanlief, and found a challenge in his regard. "It seems," she admitted, "as if—I hardly like to say it,—but it seems as if there was no soul in him any more. He is a shell, a husk. The life in him seems purely muscular. It is very depressing. Why do you think you can do anything for Clarence, Professor? I did not know your researches took you into medicine?"

"Ah, but you admit this is not a matter for medicine, but for the mind. Will you allow me an experiment madame? I give you my word of honor, my honor and my reputation, that there is no risk, and there may be—perhaps, an entire restoration. There is—a certain operation that I wish to try—"

"An operation? The most eminent doctors have told me such a thing would be useless. We might as well leave my poor husband clear of the knife, Professor."

"Oh, it is no operation, in that sense. Nothing surgical. I can hardly explain; professional secrets are involved. If you did not know that I am but a plodding old man of science—if I were an unknown charlatan—I would not ask you to put faith in me. But—I give you my word, my promise, that if you will let Mr. Wentworth come with me in my brougham I will return with him within the hour. He will be either as he is now, or—as he once was."

"As he once was—!" Mrs. Wentworth repeated the phrase, and the thought brought her a keen moment of anguish that left a visible impress on her features. "Ah," she sighed, "if I could only think such a thing possible!" She brooded in silence a moment or two. Then she spoke.

"Very well. You will find him in the library. Prim, show the gentleman to the library. If you can persuade him, Professor—" She smiled bitterly. "But then, anybody can persuade him nowadays." She turned to some embroidery as if to dismiss the subject, to show that she was resigned even to hopeless experiments. The very fact that she was plying the needle rather than the social sceptre was gauge of her descent from the heights. As a matter of fact Vanlief found Wentworth amenable enough. Wentworth was reading Marie Corelli. His mind was as empty as that. Nothing could better define his utter lapse from intelligence. He put the book down reluctantly as the Professor came in. He listened without much enthusiasm. A drive? Why not? He hadn't driven much of late, but if it was something that would please the Professor. He remembered, through a mist, that he had known Vanlief when he himself was a boy; his father had often spoken of Vanlief with respect. Nothing further in the way of mental exertion came to him. He followed Vanlief as a dog follows whoso speaks kindly to it.

The conversation between the two, in the brougham, would hardly tend to the general entertainment. It was a thing of shreds and patches. It led nowhither.

The brougham stopped at the door of Orson Vane's house. Nevins let them in, whispering an assuring confidence to the professor. As they reached the door of the dressing-room Vanlief pushed Wentworth ahead of him, and bade him enter. He kept behind him, letting the other's body screen him from the staring mirror.

Wentworth looked at himself. A hand traveled slowly up to his forehead.

"By Jove!" he said, hesitatingly, "I never put the curtain back, after all." And he covered up the mirror. "Curious thing," he went on, with energy vitalizing each word, "what possessed me to come here just now, when I know for a fact that they're playing the Inter-State Golf championships to-day. Dashed if I know why I didn't go!" He walked out, plainly puzzled, clumsily heedless of Vanlief and Nevins, but—himself once more.

Orson Vane, at just that time, was on the links of the Fifeshire Golf Club. He was wearing a little red coat with yellow facings. He was in the act of stooping on a green, to look along the line of his putt, when he got to his feet in a hurried, bewildered way. He threw his putter down on the green. He blushed all over, shaming the tint of his scarlet coat.

"What a foolish game for a grown-up man!" he blurted out, and strode off the grounds.

The bystanders were aghast. They could not find words. Orson Vane, the very prophet of golf, to throw it over in that fashion! It was inexplicable! The episode was simply maddening.

But it was remarked that the decline of golf on this side of the water dated from that very day.

CHAPTER XII.

Orson Vane was taking lunch with Professor Vanlief. Jeannette, learning of Vane's coming, had absented herself.

"It is true," Vane was saying, "that I can assert what no other man has asserted before,—that I know the exact mental machinery of two human beings. Yes; that is quite true. But—"

"I promised nothing more," remarked Vanlief.

"No. That is true, too. I have lived the lives of others; I have given their thoughts a dwelling. But I am none the happier for that."

"Oh," admitted Vanlief, "wisdom does not guarantee happiness...." He drummed with his fine, long fingers, upon the table-cloth. Vane, watching him, noted the almost transparent quality of his skin. Under that admirable mask of military uprightness there was an aging, a fading process going on, that no keen observer could miss. "It is the pursuit, not the capture of wisdom, that brings happiness. Wisdom is too often only a bubble that bursts when you touch it."

"Perhaps that is it. At any rate I know that I do not love my neighbor any more because I have fathomed some of his thoughts. Moreover, Professor, has it occurred to you that your discovery, your secret, carries elements of danger with it? Take my own experiments; there might have been tragic results; whole lives might have been ruined. In one case I was nearly the victim of a tragedy myself; I might have become, for all time, the dreadful creature I was giving house-room to. In the other, there was no more than a farce possible; the visiting spirit was, after all, in subjection to my own. I think you will have to simplify the details of your marvelous secret. It works a little clumsily, a little—"

"Oh," the Professor put in, "I am perfecting the process. I spend my days and my nights in elaborating the details. I mean to have it in the simplest, most unmistakable perfection before I hand it over to the human race."

"Sometimes I think," mused Vane, "that your boon will be a doubtful one. I can see no good to be gained. My whole point of view is changing. I ached for such a chance of wisdom once; now that it has come to me I am sad because the things I have learned are so horrible, so silly. I had not thought there were such souls in the world; or not, at any rate, in the immediate world about me."

"Oh," the Professor went on, steadfastly, "there will be many benefits in the plan. Doctors will be able to go at once to the root of any ailments that have their seat in the brain. Witnesses cab be made to testify the truth. Oh—there are ever so many possibilities."

"As many for evil as for good. Second-rate artists could steal the ideas, the inventions of others. No inventor, no scientist, would be sure of keeping his secrets. The thing would be a weapon in the hands of the unscrupulous."

"Ah, well," smiled Vanlief, "so far I have not made my discovery public, have I? It is a thing I must consider very carefully. As you say, there are arguments on either side. But you must bear in mind that you are somewhat embittered. It was your own fault; you chose the subject wittingly. If you were to read a really beautiful mind, you might turn to the other extreme; you might urge me to lose no time in giving the world my secret. The wise way is between the two; I must go forward with my plans, prepared for either course. I may take it to my grave with me, or I may give it to the world; but, so far, it is still a little incomplete; it is not ripe for general distribution. Instead of the one magic mirror there must be myriads of them. There are stupendous opportunities. All that you have told me of your own experiences in these experiments has proved my skill to have been wisely employed; your success was beyond my hopes. Do you think you will go on?"

Orson Vane did not answer at once. It was something he had been asking himself; he was not yet sure of the answer.

"I haven't made up my mind," he replied. "So far I have hardly been repaid for my time and the vital force employed. I almost feel toward these experiments as toward a vice that refines the mind while coarsening the frame. That is the story of the most terrible vices, I think; they corrode the body while gilding the brain. But this much I know; if I use your mirror again it will not be to borrow a merely smart soul; I mean to go to some other sphere of life. That one is too contracted."

"Strange," said the Professor, "that you should have said that. Jeannette pretends she thinks that, too. I cannot get her to take her proper position in the world. She is a little elusive. But then, to be sure, she is not, just now, at her best."

"She is not ill?" asked Vane, with a guilty start.

"Nothing tangible. But not—herself...."

Vane observed that he wished he might have found her in; he feared he had offended her; he hoped the Professor would use his kind offices again to soften the young lady's feelings toward him. Then he got up to go.

Strolling along the avenue he noted certain aspects of the town with an appreciation that he had not always given them. He had seen these things from so many other points of view of late; had been in sympathy with them, had made up a fraction of their more grotesque element; that to see them clearly with his own eyes had a sort of novelty. The life of to-day, as it appeared on the smartest surfaces, was, he reflected, a colorful if somewhat soulless picture....

The young men sit in the clubs and in the summer casinos, smoking and wondering what the new mode in trousers is to be; an acquaintance goes by; he has a hat that is not quite correct, and his friends comment on it yawningly; he has not the faintest notion of polite English, but nobody cares; a man who has written great things walks by, but he wears a creased coat, and the young men in the smoking-room sniff at him. In the drags and the yachts the women and the girls sit in radiance and gay colors and arrogant unconsciousness of position and power; they talk of golfing and fashion and mustachios; Mrs. Blank is going a hot pace and Mrs. Landthus is a thoroughbred; adjectives in the newest sporting slang fly about blindingly; the language is a curious argot, as distinct as the tortuous lingo of the Bowery. A coach goes rattling by, the horses throwing their heads in air, and their feet longing for the Westchester roads. The whip discusses bull-terriers; the people behind him are declaring that the only thing you can possibly find in the Waldorf rooms is an impossible lot of people. The complexions of all these people, intellectually presentable in many ways, and fashionable in yet more modes, are high in health. They look happy, prosperous and satisfied....

Yes, there was a superficial fairness to the picture, Vane admitted. If only, if only, he had not chosen to look under the surface! Now that he had seen the world with other eyes, its fairness could rarely seem the same to him.

A sturdy beggar approached him, with a whine that proved him an admirable actor. But Vane could not find it in him to reflect that if there is one thing more than another that lends distinction to a town it is an abundance of beggars.

He wondered how it would be to annex this healthy impostor's mite of a soul. But no; there could be little wisdom gained there.

He made, finally, for the Town and Country Club, and tried to immerse himself in the conversation that sped about. The talked turned to the eminent actor, Arthur Wantage. The subject of that man's alleged eccentricities invariably brought out a flood of the town's stalest anecdotes. Vane, listening in a lazy mood, made up his mind to see Wantage play that night. It would be a distraction. It would show him, once again, the present limit in one human being's portraiture of another; he would see the highest point to which external imitation could be brought; he could contrast it with the heights to which he himself had ascended.

It would be a chance for him to consider Wantage, for the first time in his life, as a merely second-rate actor. This player was an adept only in the making the shell, the husk, seem lifelike; since he could not read the character, how could he go deeper?

The opportunities the theatre held for him suddenly loomed vast before Vane.

CHAPTER XIII.

The fact that Arthur Wantage was to be seen and heard, nightly, in a brilliant comedy by the author of "Pious Aeneas," was not so much the attraction that drew people to his theatre, as was the fact that he had not yet, that season, delivered himself of a curtain speech. His curtain speeches were wont to be insults delivered in an elaborately honeyed manner; he took the pose of considering his audiences with contempt; he admired himself far more for his condescension in playing to them than he respected his audiences for having the taste to admire him.

The comedy in which he was now appearing was the perfection of paradox. It pretended to be frivolous and was really philosophic. The kernel of real wisdom was behind the elaborately poised mask of wit. A delightful impertinence and exaggeration informed every line of the dialogue. The pose of inimitable, candid egoism showed under every situation. The play was typical of the author as well as of the player. It veiled, as thinly as possible, a deal of irony at the expense of the play going public; it took some of that public's dearest foibles and riddled them to shreds.

It was currently reported that the only excuse for comparatively amicable relations between Wantage and O'Deigh, who had written this comedy, was the fact of there being an ocean between them. Even at that Wantage found it difficult to suffer the many praises he heard bestowed, not upon himself but O'Deigh. He had burst out in spleen at this adulation, once, in the hearing of an intimate.

"My dear Arthur," said the other, "you strike me as very ungrateful. For my part, when I see your theatre crowded nightly, when I see how your exchequer fills steadily, it occurs to me that you should go down on your knees every night, and thank God that O'Deigh has done you such a stunning play."

"Oh," was Wantage's grudging answer, "I do, you know I do. But I also say: Oh, God, why did it have to be by O'Deigh?"

The secret of his hatred for O'Deigh was the secret of his hatred for all dramatists. He was a curious compound of egoism, childishness and shrewdness. Part of his shrewdness—or was it his childishness?—showed in his aversion to paying authors' royalties. He always tried to re-write all the plays he accepted; if the playwrights objected there was sure to be a row of some sort. When he could find no writers willing to make him a present of plays, for the sake, as he put it, of having it done by as eminent an actor as himself, and in so beautiful a theatre, he was in the habit of announcing that he would forsake the theatre, and turn critic. He pretended that the world—the public, the press, even the minor players—were in league against him. There was a conspiracy to drive him from the theatre; the riff-raff resented that a man of genius should be so successful. They lied about him; he was sure they lied; for stories, of preposterous import, came to him; he vowed he never read the newspapers—never. As for London—oh, he could spin you the most fascinating yarn of the cabal that had dampened his London triumph. He mentioned, with a world of meaning in his tone, the name of the other great player of the time; he insinuated that to have him, Wantage, succeed in London, had not been to that other player's mind; so the wires had been pulled; oh, it was all very well done. He laughed at the reminiscence,—a brave, bluff laugh, that told you he could afford to let such petty jealousies amuse him.

The riddle of Arthur Wantage's character had never yet been read. There were those who averred he was never doing anything but acting, not in the most intimate moments of his life; some called him a keen moneymaker, retaining the mummer's pose off the stage for the mere effect of it on the press and the public. What the man's really honest, unrehearsed thoughts were,—or if he ever had such—no man could say. To many earnest students of life this puzzle had presented itself. It began to present itself, now, to Orson Vane.

This, surely, was a secret worth the reading. Here were, so to say, two masks to lift at once. This man, Arthur Wantage, who came out before the curtain now as this, now as that, character of fancy or history, what shred of vital, individual personality had he retained through all these changings? The enthusiasm of discovery, of adventure came upon Vane with a sharpness that he had not felt since the day he had mocked the futility of human science because it could not unlock other men's brains.

The horseshoe-shaped space that held the audience glittered with babble and beauty as Orson Vane took his seat in the stalls. The presence of the smart set gave the theatre a very garland of charm, of grace, and of beauty's bud and blossom. The stalls were radiant, and full of polite chatter. The boxes wore an air of dignified twilight,—a twilight of goddesses. The least garish of the goddesses, yet the one holding the subtlest sway, was Jeanette Vanlief. She sat, in the shadow of an upper box, with her father and Luke Moncreith. On her pale face the veins showed, now and then; the flush of rose came to it like a surprise—like the birth of a new world. She radiated no obvious, blatant fascination. Her hands slim and white; her voice firm and low; her eyes of a hue like that of bronze, streaked like the tiger-lilies; her profile sharp as a cameo's; the nose, with its finely-chiseled nostrils, curved in Roman mode; the mouth, thin and of the faintest possible red, slightly drooping. And then, her hair! It held, again, a spray of lilies of the valley; the artificial lights discovered in the waves and the curls of it the most unexpected shades, the most mercurial tints. The slight touch of melancholy that hovered over her merely enhanced her charm. Moncreith told himself that he would go to the uttermost ends of evil to win this woman. He had come, the afternoon of that day, through the most dangerous stream in the world, the stream of loveliness that flows over certain portions of the town at certain fashionable hours. It is a stream the eddies of which are of lace and silk; its pools are the blue of eye and the rose of mouth; its cataracts are skirts that swirl and whisper and sing of ivory outlines and velvet shadows. Yet, as he looked at Jeannette Vanlief, all that fascinating, dangerous stream lost its enticement for him; he saw her as a dream too high for comparison with the mere earthiness of the town. He felt, with a grim resolution, that nothing human should come between him and Jeannette.

Orson Vane, from his chair, paid scant attention to his fellow spectators. He was intent upon the dish that O'Deigh and Wantage had prepared for his delectation. He felt a delicious interest in every line, every situation. He had made up his mind that he would go to the root of the mystery that men called Arthur Wantage. Whether that mask concealed a real, high intelligence, or a mere, cunning, monkeylike facility in imitation—his was to be the solution of that question. Wrapped up in that thought he never so much as glanced toward the box where his friends sat.

At the end of the first act Vane strolled out into the lobby. He nodded hither and thither, but he felt no desire for nearer converse. A hand on his shoulder brought him face to face with Professor Vanlief. He was asked to come up to the box. He listened, gravely, to the Professor's words, and thanked him. So Moncreith was smitten? He smiled in a kindly way; he understood, now, the many brusqueries of his friend. That day, long ago, when he had been so inexplicable in the little bookshop; the many other occasions, since then, when Luke had been rude and bitter. A man in love was never to be reckoned on. He wished Luke all the luck in the world. It struck him but faintly that he himself had once longed for that sweet daughter of Augustus Vanlief's; he told himself that it was a dream he must put away. He was a mariner bent on many deep-sea voyages and many hazards of fate; it would be unfair to ask any woman to share in any such life. His life would be devoted to furthering the Professor's discoveries; he meant to be an adventurer into the regions of the human soul; it was a land whither none could follow.

Perhaps, if he had seen Jeannette, he might have felt no such resignation. His mood was so tense in its devotion to the puzzle presented by the player, Wantage, that the news brought him by Vanlief did not suffice to rouse him. He had a field of his own; that other one he was content to leave to Moncreith.

Moncreith, in the meanwhile, was making the most of the opportunity the Professor, in the kindness of his heart, had given him. The orchestra was playing a Puccini potpourri. It rose feebly against the prattle and the chatter and the hissing of the human voices. Moncreith, at first, found only the most obvious words.

"A trifle bitter, the play," he said, "rather like a sneer, don't you think?"

"Well," granted Jeannette, indolently, "I suppose it is not called 'Voltaire' for nothing. And there are moods that such a play might suit."

"No doubt. But—do you think one can be bitter, when one loves?"

The girl looked up in wonder. She blushed. The melancholy did not leave her face. "Bitter? Love?" she echoed. "They spell the same thing."

"Oh," he urged, "the play has made you morbid. As for me, I have heard nothing, seen nothing, but you. The bitterness of the play has skimmed by me, that is all; I have been in too sweet a dream to let those people on the stage—"

"How Wantage would rage if he heard you," said the girl. She felt what was coming, and she meant to fence as well as she could to avoid it.

"Wantage? Bother Wantage!" He leaned down to her, and whispered, "Jeannette!"

The flush on her cheek deepened, but she did not stir. It was as if she had not heard. She shut her eyes. All her weapons dropped at once. She knew it had to come; she knew, too, that, in this crisis, her heart stood plainly legible to her. Moncreith's name was not there.

"Jeannette," Moncreith went on, in his vibrant whisper, "don't you guess what dream I have been living in for so long? Don't you know that it is you, you, you—" He faltered, his emotions outstriding his words. "It is you," he finished, "that spell happiness for me. I—oh, is there no other, less crude way of putting it?—I love you, Jeannette! And you?"

He waited. The chattering and light laughter in the stalls and throughout the house seemed to lull into a mere hushed murmur, like the fluttering and twittering of a thousand birds. Moncreith, in his tense expectation, had heed only for the face of the girl beside him. He did not see, in the aisle below, Orson Vane, sauntering to his seat. He did not follow the direction of Jeannette Vanlief's eyes, the instant before she turned, and answered.

"I wish you had not spoken. I can't say anything—anything that you would like. Please, please—" She shook her head, in evident distress.

"Ah," he burst out, "then it is true, after all, what I have feared. It is true that you prefer that—that—"

She stayed him with a quick look.

"I did not say I preferred anyone. I simply said that you must consider the question closed. I am sorry, oh, so sorry. I wish a man and a woman could ever be friends, in this world, without risking either love or hate."

"All the same," he muttered, fiercely, "I believe you prefer that fellow—"

"Orson Vane's downstairs," said the Professor entering the box at that moment.

"That damned chameleon!" So Moncreith closed, under his breath, his just interrupted speech.

CHAPTER XIV.

A little before the end of that performance of "Voltaire," Orson Vane made his way to Arthur Wantage's dressing-room. They had, in their character of men in some position of eminence in different phases of the town's life, a slight acquaintance. They met, now and then, at the Mummers' Club. Vane's position put him above possibility of affront by Wantage in even the most arrogant and mannerless of the latter's moods.

Vane's invitation to a little supper, a little chat, and a little smoke, just for the duet of them, brought forth Wantage's most winning smile of acquiescence.

"Delighted, dear chap," he vowed. He could be, when he chose, the most winning of mortals. He was, during the drive to Vane's house, an admirable companion. He told stories, he made polite rejoinders, he was all glitter and graciousness. But it was when he was seated to an appetizing little supper that he became most splendid.

"My dear Vane," he said, lifting a glass to the light, "you should write me a play. I am sure you could do it. These fellows who are in the mere business of it,—well, they are really impossible. They are so vulgar, so dreadful to do business with. I hate business, I am a child in such affairs; everyone cheats me. I mean to have none but gentlemen on my business staff next season. The others grate on me, Vane, they grate. And if I could only gather a company of actors who were also gentlemen—Oh, I assure you, one cannot believe what things I endure. The stupidity of actors!" He pronounced the word as if it were accented on the last syllable. He raised his eyes to heaven as he faltered in description of the stupidities he had to contend with.

"Write a play?" said Orson, "I fear that would be out of my line. I merely live, you know; I do not describe."

"Oh, I think you would be just the man. You would give me a play that society would like. You would make no mistakes of taste. And think, my dear fellow, just think of the prestige my performance would give you. It would be the making of you. You would be launched. You would need no other recommendation. When you approach any of these manager fellows all you have to do is to say, 'Wantage is doing a play of mine.' That is a hallmark; it means success for a young man."

"Perhaps. But I have no ambitions in that way. How do you like my Bonnheimer?"

"H'm—not bad, Vane, not bad. But you should taste my St. Innesse. It is a '74. I got it from the cellars of the Duke of Arran. You know Merrill, the wine-merchant on Broadway? Shrewd fellow! Always keeps me in mind; whenever he sees a sale of a good cellar on the other side, he puts in a bid; knows he can always depend on Wantage taking the bouquet of it off his hands. You must take dinner with me some night, and try that St. Innesse. Ex-President Richards told me, the other evening, that it was the mellowest vintage he had tasted in years. You know Richards? Oh, you should, you should!"

Vane listened, quietly amused. The vanity, the egoism of this player were so obvious, so transparent, so blatant. He wondered, more than ever, what was under that mask of arrogance and conceit. The perfect frankness of the conceit made it almost admirable.

"You know," Wantage remarked presently, "I'm really playing truant, taking supper with you. I ought to be studying."

"A new play?"

"No. My curtain speech for to-morrow night. It's the last night of the season, and they expect it of me, you know. I've vowed, time and again, I would never make another curtain-speech in my life, but they will have them, they will have them!" He sighed, in submission to his fate. Then he returned to a previous thought. "I wish, though," he said, "that I could persuade you to do a play for me. Think it over! Think of the name it would give you. Or you might try managing me. Eh, how does that strike you? Such a relief to me if I could deal with a gentleman. You have no idea—the cads there are in the theatre! They resent my being a man who tries to prove a little better educated than themselves. They hate me because I am college-bred, you know; they prefer actors who never read. How many books do you think I read before I attempted Voltaire? A little library, I tell you. And then the days I spent in noting the portraits! I traveled France in my search. For the actor who takes historic characters there cannot be too many documents. Imagination alone is not enough. And then the labor of making the play presentable; I wish you could see the thing as it first came to me! You would think a man like O'Deigh would have taken into consideration the actor? But no; the play, as O'Deigh left it, might have been for a stock company. Frederick the Great was as fine a part as my own. Oh, they are numbskulls. And the rehearsals! Actors are sheep, simply sheep. The papers say I am a brute at rehearsals. My dear Vane, I swear to you that if Nero were in my place he would massacre all the minor actors in the land. And they expect the salaries of intelligent persons!"

Vane, listening, wondered why Wantage, under such an avalanche of irritations, continued such life. Gradually it dawned on him that all this fume and fret was merely part of the man's mummery; it was his appeal to the sympathy of his audience; his argument against the reputation his occasional exhibitions of rage and waywardness had given him.

Vane's desire to penetrate the surface of this conscious imitator, this fellow who slipped off this character to assume that, grew keener and keener. Where, under all this crust of alien form and action, was the individual, human thought and feeling? Or was there any left? Had the constant corrosion of simulated emotions burnt out all the original character of the mind?

Vane could not sufficiently hasten the end for which he had invited Wantage.

"You are," he said presently, as a lull in the other's monologue allowed him an opening, "something of an amateur of tapestry, of pictures, of bijouterie. I have a little thing or two, in my dressing-room, that I wish you would give me an opinion on."

They took their cigarettes into the adjoining dressing-room. Wantage went, at once, to the mirrors.

"Ah, Florence, I see." He frowned, in critical judgment; he went humming about the room, singing little German phrases to the pictures, snatches of chansonettes to the tapestries. He was very enjoyable as a spectacle, Vane told himself. He tiptoed over the room, now in the mode of his earliest success, "The King of Dandies," now in the half limping style of his "Rigoletto."

"You should have seen the Flemish things I had!" he declared. That was his usual way of noting the belongings of others; they reminded him of his own superior specimens. "I sold them for a song, at auction. Don't you think one tires of one's surroundings, after a time? People go to the hills and the seashore, because they tire of town. I have the same feeling about pictures, and furniture, and bric-a-brac. After a time, they tire me. I have to get rid of them. I sell them at auction. People are always glad to bid for something that has belonged to Arthur Wantage. But everything goes for a song. Oh, it is ruinous, ruinous." He peered, and pirouetted about the corners. "Ah," he exclaimed, "and here is something covered up! A portrait? Something rare?" He posed in front of it, affecting the most devouring curiosity.

"A sort of portrait," said Vane, touching the cord at back of the mirror.

"Ah," said Wantage, gazing, "you are right. A sort of portrait." And he laughed, feebly, feebly. "That Bonnheimer," he muttered, "a deuce of a wine!" He clutched at a chair, reeling into it.

Vane, passing to the mirror's face, took what image it turned to him, and then, leisurely, replaced the curtain.

He surveyed the figure in the chair for a moment or so. Then he called Nevins. "Nevins," he said, "where the devil are you? Never where you're wanted. What does one pay servants outrageous wages for! They conspire to cheat one, they all do. Nevins!" Nevins appeared, wide-eyed at this outburst. He was prepared for many queer exhibitions on the part of his master, but this—this, to a faithful servant! He stood silent, expectant, reproachful.

"Nevins," his master commanded, "have this—this actor put to bed. Use the library; make the two couches serve. He'll stay here for twenty-four hours; you understand, twenty-four hours. You will take care of him. The wine was badly corked, to-night, Nevins. You grow worse every day. You are in league to drive me distracted. It is an outrage. Why do you stand there, and shake, in that absurd fashion? It makes me quite nervous. Do go away, Nevins, go away!"

CHAPTER XV.

The papers of that period are all agreed that the eminent actor, Arthur Wantage, was never seen to more advantage than on the last night of that particular season. His Voltaire had never been a more brilliant impersonation. The irony, the cruelty of the character had rarely come out more effectively; the ingenuity of the dialogue was displayed at its best.

Yet, as a matter of fact, Arthur Wantage, all that day and evening, was in Orson Vane's house, subject to a curious mental and spiritual aphasia that afterwards became a puzzle to many famous physicians.

The Voltaire was Orson Vane.

It was the final triumph of Professor Vanlief's thaumaturgy. Vane was now in possession of the entire mental vitality sufficient for playing the part of the evening; the lines, the every pose, came to him spontaneously, as if he were machinery moving at another's guidance. The detail of entering the theatre unobserved had been easy; it was dusk and he was muffled to the eyes. Afterwards, it was merely a matter of pigment and paints. His fingers found the use of the colors and powders as easily as his mind held the words to be spoken. There was not a soul, in the company, in the audience, that did not not find the Voltaire of that night the Voltaire of the entire season.

Above the mere current of his speeches and his displayed emotions Orson Vane found a tide of exaltation bearing him on to a triumphant feeling of contempt for his audience. These sheep, these herdlings, these creatures of the fashion, how fine it was to fling into their faces the bitter taunts of a Voltaire, to see them take them smilingly, indulgently. They paid him his price, and he hated them for it. He felt that they did not really understand the half of the play's delicate finesse; he felt their appreciation was a sham, a pose, a bit of mummery even more contemptible than his own, since they paid to pose, while he, at least, had the satisfaction of their money.

The curtain-fall found him aglow with the splendor of his success. The two personalties in him joined in a fever of triumph. He, Orson Vane, had been Voltaire; he would yet be all the other geniuses of history. He would prove himself the greatest of them all, since he could simulate them all. A certain vein of petty cunning ran under the major emotion; Orson Vane laughed to think how he had despoiled Arthur Wantage of his very temperament, his art, his spirit. This same cunning admonished, too, the prompt return of Wantage's person, after the night was over, to the Wantage residence.

The commotion "in front" brought Orson to a sense of the immediate moment. The cries for a speech came over a crackling of hand-claps. He waited for several minutes. It was not well to be too complaisant with one's public. Then he gave the signal to the man at the curtain, and moved past him, to the narrow space behind the lights. He bowed. It had the very air of irony, had that bow. It does not seem humanly possible to express irony in a curving in the spine, a declension of the head, a certain pose of the hands, but Vane succeeded, just as Wantage had so often succeeded, in giving that impression. The bow over, he turned to withdraw. Let them wait, let them chafe I Commuters were missing the last trains for the night? So much the better! They would not forget him so easily.

When he finally condescended to stride before the curtain again, it was a lift of the eyebrows, a little gesture, an air that said, quite plainly: Really, it is very annoying of you. If I were not very gracious indeed I should refuse to come out again. I do so, I assure you, under protest.

He gave a little, delicate cough, he lifted his eyes. At that the house became still, utterly still.

He began without any vocative at all.

"The actor," he said, "who wins the applause of so distinguished a company is exceedingly fortunate. The applause of such a very distinguished company—" he succeeded in emphasizing his phrase to the point where it became a subtle insult—"is very sweet to the actor. It reconciles him to what he must take to be a breach of true art, the introduction of his own person on the scene where he has appeared as an impersonator of character. Some actors are expected to make speeches after their exertions should be over. I am one of those poor actors. In the name of myself, a poor actor, and the poor actors in my company, I must thank this distinguished body of ladies and gentlemen for the patience with which they have listened to Mr. O'Deigh's little trifle. It is, of course, merely a trifle, pour passer le temps. Next season, I hope, I may give you a really serious production. Mr. O'Deigh cables me that he is happy such distinguished persons in such a critical town have applauded his little effort. I am sure ever so many of you would rather be at home than listening to the apologies of a poor actor. For I feel I must apologize for presenting so inconsiderable a trifle. A mere summer night's amusement. I have played it as a sort of rest for myself, as preparation for larger productions. If I have amused you, I am pleased. The actors' province is to please. The poor actor thanks you."

He bowed, and the bewildered company who had heard him to the end, clapped their hands a little. The newspaper men smiled at one another; they had been there before. The old question of "Why does he do it?" no longer stirred in them. They were used to Wantage's vagaries.

The newspapers of the following day had Wantage's speech in full. The critics wrote editorials on the necessity for curbing this player's arrogance. The public was astonished to find that it had been insulted, but it took the press' word for it. Wantage had made that sort of thing the convention; it was the fashion to call these curtain speeches an insult, yet to invoke them as eagerly as possible. The widespread advertising that accrued to Wantage from this episode enabled his manager to obtain, in his bookings for the following season, an even higher percentage than usual. To that extent Orson Vane's imitation of an imitator benefited his subject. In other respects it left Wantage a mere walking automaton.

It was fortunate that the closing time for Wantage's theatre was now on. There was no hitch in Vane's plan of transporting Wantage to his home quarters; the servants at the Wantage establishment found nothing unusual in their master having been away for a day and a night; he was too frequently in the habit, when his house displeased him in some detail, to stay at hotels for weeks and months at a time; his household was ready for any vagary. Indisposition was nothing new with him, either; in reality and affectation these lapses from well-being were not infrequent with the great player. The doctor told him he needed rest—rest and sea-air; there was nothing to worry over; he had been working too hard, that was all.

So the shell of what had been Wantage proceeded to a watering-place, while the kernel, now a part of Orson Vane, proceeded to astonish the town with its doings and sayings.

Practice had now enabled Vane to control, with a certain amount of consciousness, whatsoever alien spirit he took to himself. Vigorous and alert as was the mumming temperament he was now in possession of, he yet contrived to exert a species of dominance over it; he submitted to it in the mode, the expression of his character, yet in the main-spring of his action he had it in subjection. He had reached, too, a plane from which he was able, more than on any of the other occasions, to enjoy the masquerade he knew himself taking part in. He realized, with a contemptuous irony, that he was playing the part of one who played many parts. The actor in him seemed, intellectually, merely a personified palimpsest; the mind was receptive, ready to echo all it heard, keen to reproduce traits and tricks of other characters.

He held in himself, to be brief, a mirror that reflected whatever crossed its face; the base of that mirror itself was as characterless, as colorless, as the mere metal and glass. Superficialities were caught with a skill that was astonishing; little tricks of manner and speech were reproduced to the very dot upon the i; yet, under all the raiment of other men's merely material attributes, there was no change of soul at all; no transformation touched the little ego-screaming soul of the actor.

The superficial, in the meanwhile, was enough to make the town gossip not a little about the newest diversions of Orson Vane. He talked, now, of nothing but the theatre and the arts allied to it. He purposed doing some little comedies at Newport in the course of the summer that was now beginning. He eyed all the smart women of his acquaintance with an air that implied either, "I wonder whether you could be cast for a girl I must make love to," or, "You would be passable in Prince Hal attire." At home, to his servants, Vane was abominable. When the dreadful champagne, that some impulse possessed him to buy of a Broadway swindler, proved as flat as the Gowanus, his language to Nevins was quite contemptible. "What," he shrieked, "do I pay you for? Tell me that! This splendid wine spoiled, spoiled, utterly unfit for a gentleman to drink, and all by your negligence. It is enough to turn one's mind. It is an outrage. A splendid wine. And now—look at it!" As a conclusion he threw the stuff in Nevins' face. Nevins made no answer at all. He wiped the sour mess from his coat with the same air of apology that he would have used had he spilt a glass himself. But his emotions were none the less. They caused him, in the privacy of the servants' quarters, to do what he had not done in years, to drop his h's. "It's the 'ost's place," said Nevins, mournfully, "to entertain his guests, and not bully the butler." Which, as a maxim, was valid enough, save that, in this special case, the guests had come to look upon Vane's treatment of the servants as part of the entertainment a dinner with him would provide.

Another distress that fell to the lot of poor Nevins was the fact that his master was become averse to the paying of bills. The profanity fell upon Nevins from both the duns and the dunned.

"The man from Basser's, Mr. Vane, sir," Nevins would announce, timidly. "Can't get him to go away at all, sir."

"Basser's, Basser's? Oh—that tailor fellow. An impudent creature, to plague me so, when I do him the honor of wearing his coats; they fit very badly, but I put up with that because I want to help the fellow on. And what is my reward? He pesters me, pesters me. Tell him—tell him anything, Nevins. Only do leave me alone; I am very busy, very nervous. I am going to write a comedy for myself. I have some water-colors to paint for Mrs. Carlos; I have a ride in the Park, and ever so many other things to do to-day, and you bother me with pestiferous tailors. Nevins, you are, you are—"

But Nevins quietly bowed himself out before he learned what new thing he was in his master's eyes.

A malady—for it surely is no less than a malady—for attempting cutting speeches at any time and place possessed Vane. Shortsightedness was another quality now obvious in him. He knew you to-day, to-morrow he looked at you with the most unseeing eyes. His voice was the most prominent organ in whatever room or club he happened to be; when he spoke none else could be intelligible. When he knew himself observed, though alone, he hummed little snatches to himself. His gait took on a mincing step. There was not a moment, not a pose of his that had not its forethought, its deliberation, its premeditated effect.

The gradual increase in the publicity that was part of the penalty of being in the smart world had made approachment between the stage and society easier than ever before. Orson Vane's bias toward the theatre did not displease the modish. Rumors as to this and that heroine of a romantic divorce having theatric intentions became frequent. The gowns of actresses were copied by the smart quite as much as the smart set's gowns were copied by actresses. The intellectual factor had never been very prominent in the social attitude toward the stage; it was now frankly admitted that good-looking men and handsome dresses were as much as one went to the theatre for. Theatrical people had a wonderful claim upon the printer's ink of the continent; society was not averse to borrowing as much of that claim as was possible. Compliments were exchanged with amiable frequence; smart people married stage favorites, and the stage looked to the smart for its recruits.

Orson Vane could not have shown his devotion to the mummeries of the stage at a better time. He gained, rather than lost, prestige.

CHAPTER XVI.

It was the fashionable bathing hour at the most exclusive summer resort on the Atlantic coast. The sand in front of the Surf Club was dotted with gaudy tents and umbrellas. Persons whom not to know was to be unknowable were picturesquely distributed about the club verandahs in wicker chairs and lounges. The eye of an artist would have been distracted by the beauties that were suggested in the half-lifted skirts of this beauty, and revealed in the bathing-suit of that one. The little waves that came politely rippling up the slope of sand seemed to know what was expected of them; they were in nowise rude. They may have longed to ruffle this or that bit of feminine frippery, but they refrained. They may have ached to drown out Orson Vane's voice as he said "good morning" to everybody in and out of the water; but they permitted themselves no such luxury.

Orson Vane was a beautiful picture as he entered the water. His suit was immaculate; a belt prevented the least wrinkle in his jersey; a rakish sombrero gave his head a sort of halo. He poised a cigarette in one hand, keeping himself afloat with the other. He bowed obsequiously to all the pretty women; he invited all the rich ones to tea and toast—"We always have a little tea and toast at my cottage on Sundays, you know; you'll meet only nice-looking people, really; we have a jolly time." Most of the men he was unable to see; the sunlight on the water did make such a glare.

On the raft Orson Vane found the only Mrs. Carlos.

"If it were not for you, Mrs. Carlos," he assured her, "the ocean would be quite unfashionable."

Mrs. Carlos smiled amiably. Speeches of that sort were part of the tribute the world was expected to pay her. She asked him if the yachts in the harbor were not too pretty for anything.

"No," said Vane, "no. Most melancholy sight. Bring up the wickedness of man, whenever I look at them. I bought a yacht you know, early in the summer. Liked her looks, made an offer, bought her. A swindle, Mrs. Carlos, an utter swindle. A disgraceful hulk. And now I can't sell her. And my cook is a rascal. Oh—don't mention yachts! And my private car, Mrs. Carlos, you cannot imagine the trials I endure over that! The railroads overcharge me, and the mob comes pottering about with those beastly cameras. Really, you know, I am thinking of living abroad. The theatre is better supported in Europe. I am thinking of devoting my life to the theatre altogether. It is the one true passion. It shows people how life should be lived; it is at once a school of morals and comportment." He peered into the water near the raft. Then he plunged prettily into the sea. "I see that dear little Imogene," he told Mrs. Carlos, as he swam off. Imogene was the little heiress of the house of Carlos; a mere schoolgirl. It was one of Vane's most deliberate appeals for public admiration, this worship of the society of children. He gamboled with all the tots and blossoms he could find. He knew them all by name; they dispelled his shortsightedness marvelously.

After a proper interval Vane appeared, in the coolest of flannels, on the verandah of the Club. He bowed to all the women, whether he knew them or not; he peered under the largest picture hats with an air that said "What sweet creature is hidden here?" as plainly as words.

Someone asked him why he had not been to the Casino the night before.

"Oh," he sighed, "I was fearfully busy."

"Busy?" The word came in a tone of reproach. A suspicion of any sort of toil will brand one more hopelessly in the smart set of America than in any other; one may pretend an occupation but one may not profess it in actuality.

"Oh, terribly busy," said Vane. "I am writing a comedy. I have decided that we must make authorship smarter than it has been. I shall sacrifice myself in that attempt. You've noticed that not one writing-chap in a million knows anything about our little world except what is not true? Yes; it's unmistakable. An entirely false impression of us is given to the world at large. The real picture of us must come from one of ourselves."

"And you will try it?"

"Yes. I shall do my very best. When it is finished I want you all to play parts in it. We must do something for the arts, you know. Why not the arts, as well as tailors and milliners? By the way, I want you all to come to my little lantern-dance to-night, on the Beaurivage. It is something quite novel. You must all come disguised as flowers. There will be no lights but Chinese lanterns. I shall have launches ready for you at the Casino landing. My cook is quite sober to-day, and the yacht is as presentable as if she were not an arrant fraud. I mean to have a dance that shall fit the history of society in America. For that reason the newspapers must know nothing about it. There can be no history where there are newspapers. I shall invite nobody who knows how to write; I am the only one whose taste I can trust. Some people write to live, and some live to write, and the worst class of all are merely dying to write. They are all barred to-night. We must try and break all the conventions. Conventions are like the strolling players: made to be broke."

He rattled on in this way, with painful efforts at brilliance, for quite a time. His hearers really considered it brilliance and listened patiently. Summer was not their season for intellectual exertion; it might be a virtue in others, in themselves it would have been a mistake.

The lantern-dance on Orson Vane's Beaurivage was, as everyone will remember, an event of exceeding picturesqueness. Mrs. Sclatersby appeared as a carnation; Mrs. Carlos as a rose. Some of the younger and divinely figured women appeared as various blossoms that necessitated imitation of part of Rosalind's costume under the trees. The slender, tapering stem of one white lily, fragrant and delicious, lingered long in the memories of the men who were there.

A sensation was caused by the arrival of Mrs. Barrett Weston. She came in a scow, seated on her automobile. A shriek of delight from the company greeted her. The weary minds of the elect were really tickled by this conceit. The automobile was arranged to imitate a crysanthemum. Just before she alighted Mrs. Barrett Weston touched a hidden lever and the automobile began to grind out a rag-time tune.

A stranger, approaching the Beaurivage at that moment, might have fancied himself in the politest ward of the most insane of asylums. But Orson Vane found it all most delightful. It was the affair of the season.

"Look," he cried, in the midst of a game of leapfrog in which a number of the younger guests had plunged with desperate glee, "there is the moon. How pitably weak she seems, against this brilliance here! It bears out the theory that art is always finer than nature, and that the theatre is more picturesque than life. Look at what we are doing, this moment! We are imitating pleasure. And will you show me any unconscious pleasure that is so delightful as this?"

By the time people had begun to feel a polite hunger Vane had completed his scheme of having several unwieldy barges brought alongside the Beaurivage. There were two of the clumsy but roomy decks on either side of the slender, shapely yacht. Over this now quite wide space the tables were arranged. While the supper went on, Orson Vane did a little monologue of his own. Nobody paid any attention, but everyone applauded.

"What a scene for a comedy," he explained, proudly surveying the picture of the gaiety before him, "what a delicious scene! It is almost real. I must write a play around it. I have quite made up my mind to devote my life to the theatre. It is the only real life. It touches the emotions at all points; it is not isolated in one narrow field of personality. Have I your permission to put you all in my play? How sweet of you! I shall have a scene where we all race in automobiles. We will be quite like dear little children who have their donkey-races. But I think automobiles are so much more intelligent than donkeys, don't you? And they have such profound voices! Have you ever noticed the intonation of the automobiles here? That one of Mrs. Barrett Weston has a delicate tenor; it is always singing love-songs as if it were tired of life. Then we have bassos, and baritones, and repulsive falsettos. My automobile has a voice like a phonograph. When it bubbles along the avenue I can hear, as plainly as anything, that it is imitating one of the other automobiles. Some automobiles, I suppose, have the true instinct for the theatre. Have you noticed how theatric some of the things are, how they contrive to run away just when everyone is looking?"

"Just like horses," murmured one of his listeners.

"Oh, no; I wouldn't say that. Horses have a merely natural intelligence; it is nothing like the splendidly artificial reasoning of the automobile. The poor horse, I really pity him! He has nothing before him but polo. But how thankful he should be to polo. He was a broncho with disreputable manners; now he is a polo-pony with a neat tail. In time, I dare say, the horse can learn some of the higher civilization of the automobile, just as society may still manage to be as intelligent as the theatre."

The conclusion of that entertainment marked the height of Orson Vane's peculiar fame. The radical newspapers caught echoes of it and invented what they could not transcribe. The young men who owned newspapers had not been invited by Orson Vane, because, in spite of his theatric mania, he had no illusions about the decency of metropolitan journalism. He avowed that the theatre might be a trifle highflavored, but it had, at the least, nothing of the hypocrisy that smothers the town in lies to-day and reads it a sermon to-morrow. The most conspicuous of these newspaper owners went into something like convulsions over what he called the degeneracy of our society. Himself most lamentably in a state of table-d'hotage, this young man trumpeted forth the most bitter editorials against Orson Vane and his doings. He frothed with anarchistic ravings. Finally, since the world will always listen if you only make noise loud enough and long enough, the general public began to believe that Vane was really a dreadful person. He was a leader in the smart set; he stood for the entire family. His taste for the theater would debauch all society. His egoisms would spoil what little of the natural was left in the regions of Vanity Fair. So went the chatter of the man-on-the-street, that mighty power, whom the most insignificant of little men-behind-the-pen can move at will.

One may be ever so immersed in affairs that are not of the world and its superficial doings, yet it is almost impossible to escape some faint echo of what the world is chattering about. Professor Vanlief, who had betaken himself and Jeanette, for the summer, to a little place in the mountains, was finally routed out of his peace by the rumors concerning Orson Vane. The give and take of conversation, even at a little farm-house in the hills, does not long leave any prominent subject untouched. So Augustus Vanlief one morning bought all the morning papers.

He found more than he had wanted. The editorials against the doings of the smart set, the reports of the sermons preached against their goings-on, were especially pregnant that morning.

In another part of the paper he found a line or two, however, that brought him sharply to a sense of necessary action. The lines were these:

Augustus Vanlief saw what no other mortal could have guessed. He saw the connection between those two newspaper items, the one about Vane and the one about Wantage.

CHAPTER XVII

Professor Vanlief lost no time in inventing an excuse for his immediate departure. Jeannette would be well looked after. He got a few necessaries together and started for Framley Lodge. After some delay he obtained an interview with the distinguished patient.

"Try," urged Vanlief, "to tell me when this illness came upon you. Was it after your curtain-speech at the end of last season?"

Wantage looked with blank and futile eyes. "Curtain-speech? I made none."

"Oh, yes. Try to remember! It made a stir, did that speech of yours. Try to think what happened that day!"

"I made no speech. I remember nothing. I am Wantage, I think. Wantage. I used to act, did I not?" He laughed, feebly. It was melancholy to watch him. He could eat and drink and sleep; he had the intelligence of an echo. Each thought of his needed a stimulant.

Vanlief persisted, in spite of melancholy rebuffs. There was so much at stake. This man's whole career was at stake. And, if matters were not mended soon, the evil would be under way; the harm would have begun. It meant loss, actual loss now, and one could scarcely compute how much ruin afterwards. And he, Vanlief, would be the secret agent of this ruin! Oh, it was monstrous! Something must be done. Yet, he could do nothing until he was sure. To meddle, without absolute certainty, would be criminal.

"What do you remember before you fell ill?" he repeated.

"Oh, leave me alone!" said Wantage. "Isn't the doctor bad enough, without you. I tell you I remember nothing. I was well, and now I am ill. Perhaps it was something Orson Vane gave me at supper that night, I don't remember—"

"At supper? Vane?" The Professor leaped at the words.

"Yes. I said so, didn't I? I had supper in his rooms, and then—"

But Vanlief was gone. He had no time for the amenities now. His age seemed to leave him as his purpose warmed, and his goal neared. All the fine military bearing came out again. The people who traveled with him that day took him for nothing less than a distinguished General.

At the end of the day he reached Vane's town house. Nevins was all alone there; all the other servants were on the Beaurivage. The man looked worn and aged. He trembled visibly when he walked; his nerves were gone, and he had the taint of spirits on him.

"Mr. Vanlief, sir," he whined, "it'll be the death of me, will this place. First he buys a yacht, sir, like I buy a 'at, if you please; and now I'm to sell the furniture and all the antics. These antics, sir, as the master 'as collected all over the world, sir. It goes to me 'eart."

Vanlief, even in his desperate mood, could not keep his smile back. "Sell the antiques, eh? Well, they'll fetch plenty, I've no doubt. But if I were you I wouldn't hurry; Mr. Vane may change his mind, you know."

"Ah," nodded Nevins, brightening, "that's true, sir. You're right; I'll wait the least bit. It's never too soon to do what you don't want to, eh, sir? And I gives you my word, as a man that's 'ad places with the nobility, sir, that the last year's been a sad drain on me system. What with swearing, sir, and letters I wouldn't read to my father confessor, sir, Mr. Vane's simply not the man he was at all. Of course, if he says to sell the furniture, out it goes! But, like as not, he'll come in here some line day and ask where I've got all his trappings. And then I'll show him his own letter, and he'll say he never wrote it. Oh, it's a bad life I've led of late, sir. Never knowing when I could call my soul my own."

The phrase struck the Professor with a sort of chill. It was true; if his discovery went forth upon the world, no man would, in very truth, know when he could call his soul his own. It would be at the mercy of every poacher. But he could not, just now, afford reflections of such wide scope; there was a nearer, more immediate duty.

"Nevins," he said, "I came about that mirror of mine."

"Yes, sir. I'm glad of that, sir; uncommon glad. You'll betaking it away, sir? It's bad luck I've 'ad since that bit of plate come in the house."

"You're right. I mean to take it away. But only for a time. Seeing Mr. Vane's thinking of selling up, perhaps it's just as well if I have this out of the way for a time, eh? Might avoid any confusion. I set store by that mirror, Nevins; I'd not like it sold by mistake."

"Well, sir, if you sets more store by it than the master, I'd like to see it done, sir. The master's made me life a burden about that there glass. I've 'ad to watch it like a cat watches a mouse. I don't know now whether I'd rightly let you take it or not." He scratched his head, and looked in some quandary.

"Nonsense, Nevins. You know it's mine as well as you know your own name. Didn't you fetch it over from my house in the first place, and didn't you pack it and wrap it under my very eyes?"

"True, sir; I did. My memory's a bit shaky, sir, these days. You may do as you like with your own, I'll never dispute that. But Mr. Vane's orders was mighty strict about the plaguey thing. I wish I may never see it again. It's been, 'Nevins, let nobody disturb the new mirror!' and 'Nevins, did anyone touch the new mirror while I was gone?' and 'Nevins, was the window open near the new mirror?' until I fair feel sick at the sight of it."

"No doubt," said the professor, impatiently. "Then you'll oblige me by wrapping it up for shipping purposes as soon as ever you can. I'm going to take it away with me at once. I suppose there's no chance of Mr. Vane dropping in here before I bring the glass back, but, if he does, tell him you acted under my orders."

"A good riddance," muttered Nevins, losing no time over his task of covering and securing the mirror. "I'll pray it never comes this way again," he remarked.

The professor, after seeing that all danger of injury to the mirror's exposed parts was over, walked nervously up and down the rooms. He would have to carry his plan through with force of arms, with sheer impertinence and energy of purpose. It was an interference in two lives that he had in view. Had he any right to that? But was he not, after all, to blame for the fact of the curious transfusion of soul that had left one man a mental wreck, and stimulated the other's forces to a course of life out of all character with the strivings of his real soul? If he had not tempted Orson Vane to these experiments, Arthur Wantage would never be drooping in the shadow of collapse, and in danger of losing his proper place in the roll of prosperity. Vanlief shuddered at thought of what an unscrupulous man might not do with this discovery of his; what lives might be ruined, what successes built on fraud and theft? Fraud and theft? Those words were foul enough in the material things of life; but how much more horrid would they be when they covered the spiritual realm. To steal a purse, in the old dramatic phrase, was a petty thing; but to steal a soul—Professor Vanlief found himself launched into a whirlpool of doubt and confusion.

He had opened a new, vast region of mental science. He had enabled one man to pass the wall with which nature had hedged the unforeseen forces of humanity. Was he to learn that, in opening this new avenue of psychic activity, he had gone counter to the eternal Scheme of Things, and let in no divine light, but rather the fierce glare of diabolism?

His thoughts traversed argument upon argument while Nevins completed his work. He heard the man's voice, finally, with an actual relief, a gladness at being recalled to the daring and doing that lay before him.

When the Professor was gone, a wagon bearing away the precious mirror, Nevins poured himself out a notably stiff glass of Five-Star.

"Here's hoping," he toasted the silent room, "the silly thing gets smashed into everlasting smithereens!"

And he drowned any fears he might have had to the contrary. This particular species of time-killing was now a daily matter with Nevins; the incessant strain upon his nerves of some months past had finally brought him to the pitch where he had only one haven of refuge left.

The Professor sped over the miles to Framley Lodge. He took little thought about meals or sleep. The excitement was marking him deeply; but he paid no heed to, or was unaware of, that. Arrived at the Lodge a campaign of bribery and corruption began. Servant after servant had to be suborned. Nothing but the well-known fame and name of Augustus Vanlief enabled him, even with his desperate expenditures of tips, to avert the suspicion that he had some deadly, some covertly inimical end in view. One does not, at this age of the world, burst into another man's house and order that man's servants about, without coming under suspicion, to put it mildly. Fortunately Vanlief encountered, just as his plot seemed shattering against the rigor of the household arrangements, the doctor who was in attendance on Wantage. The man happened to be on the staff of the University where Vanlief held a chair. He held the older man in the greatest respect; he listened to his rapid talk with all the patience in the world. He looked astonished, even uncomprehending, but he shook his shoulders up and down a few times with complaisance. "There seems no possible harm," he assented.

"Don't ask me to believe in the curative possibilities, Professor; but—there can be no harm, that I see. He is not to be unduly excited. A mirror, you say? You don't think vanity can send a man from illness to health, do you? Not even an actor can be as vain as that, surely. However, I shall tell the attendants to see that the thing is done as quietly as possible. I trust you, you see, to let nothing detrimental happen. I have to get over to the Port of Pines. I shall give the orders. Goodbye. I wish I could see the result of your little—h'm, notion—but I dare say to-morrow will be soon enough."

And he smiled the somewhat condescending smile of the successful practitioner who fancies he is addressing a campaigner whose usefulness is passing.

The setting up of the professor's mirror, so as to face Wantage's sickbed, took no little time, no little care, no little exertion. When it was in place, the professor tiptoed to the actor's side.

"Well," queried Wantage, "what is it? Medicine? Lord, I thought I'd taken all there was in the world. Where is it?"

"No," said the professor, "not medicine. I am going to ask you to look quite hard at that curtain by the foot of the bed for a moment. I have something I think may interest you and—"

As the actor's eyes, in mere physical obedience to the other's suggestion, took the desired direction, Vanlief tugged at a cord that rolled the curtain aside, revealing the mirror, which gave Wantage back the somewhat haggard apparition of himself.

A few seconds went by in silence. Then Wantage frowned sharply.

"Gad," he exclaimed, vigorously and petulantly, "what a beastly bad bit of make-up!"

The voice was the voice of the man whom the town had a thousand times applauded as "The King of the Dandies."

An exceedingly bad quarter of an hour followed for Vanlief. Wantage, now in full possession of all his mental faculties, abused the Professor up hill and down dale. What was he doing there? What business had that mirror there? What good was a covered-up mirror? Where were the servants? The doctor had given orders? The doctor was a fool. Only the mere physical infirmity consequent upon being bedridden for so long prevented Wantage from becoming violent in his rage. Vanlief, sharp as was his sense of relief at the success of his venture, was yet more relieved when his bribes finally got his mirror and himself out of the Lodge. The incident had its humors, but he was too tired, too enervated, to enjoy them. The very moment of Wantage's recovery of his soul had its note of ironic comedy; the succeeding vituperation from the restored actor; Vanlief's own meekness; the marvel and rapacity of the servants—all these were abrim with chances for merriment. But Vanlief found himself, for, perhaps, the first time in his life, too old to enjoy the happy interpretations of life. Into all his rejoicings over the outcome of this affair there crept the constant doubts, the ceaseless questionings, as to whether he had discovered a mine of wisdom and benefit, or a mere addition to man's chances for evil.

His return journey, his delivery of the mirror into Nevins' unwilling care, were accomplished by him in a species of daze.

He had hardly counted upon the danger of his discovery. Was he still young enough to contend with them?

Nevins almost flung the mirror to its accustomed place. He unwrapped it spitefully. When he left the room, the curtain of the glass was flapping in the wind. Nevins heard the sound quite distinctly; he went to the sideboard and poured out a brimming potion.

"I 'opes the wind'll play the Old 'Arry with it," he smiled to himself. He smiled often that night; he went to bed smiling. His was the cheerful mode of intoxication.

Augustus Vanlief reached the cottage in the hills a sheer wreck. He had left it a hale figure of a man who had ever kept himself keyed up to the best; now he was old, shaking, trembling in nerves and muscles.

Jeannette rushed toward him and put her arms around him. She looked her loving, silent wonder into his weary eyes.

"Sleep, dear, sleep," said this old, tired man of science, "first let me sleep."

CHAPTER XVIII.

Orson Vane, scintillating theatrically by the sea, was in a fine rage when Nevins ceased to answer his telegrams. Telegrams struck Vane as the most dramatic of epistles; there was always a certain pictorial effect in tearing open the envelope, in imagining the hushed expectation of an audience. A letter—pooh! A letter might be anything from a bill to a billet. But a telegram! Those little slips of paper struck immediate terror, or joy, or despair, or confusion; they hit hard, and swiftly. Certainly he had been hitting Nevins hard enough of late. He had peppered him with telegrams about the furniture, about the pictures; he had forbidden one day what he had ordered the day before. It never occurred to him that Nevins might seek escape from these torments. Yet that was what Nevins had done. He had tippled himself into a condition where he signed sweetly for each telegram and put it in the hall-rack. They made a beautiful, yellow festoon on the mahogany background.

"Those," Nevins told himself, "is for a gentleman as is far too busy to notice little things like telegrams."

Nevins watched that yellow border growing daily with fresh delight.

He could keep on accepting telegrams just as long as the sideboard held its strength. Each new arrival from the Western Union drove him to more glee and more spirits—of the kind one can buy bottled.

At last Orson Vane felt some alarm creeping through his armor of dramatic pose. Could Nevins have come to any harm? It was very annoying, but he would have to go to town for a day or so. That seemed unavoidable. Just as he had made up his mind to it, he happened to slip on a bit of lemon-peel. At once he fell into a towering rage. He cursed the entire service on the Beaurivage up hill and down dale. You could hear him all over the harbor. It was the voice of a profane Voltaire.

That night, at the Casino, his rage found vent in action. He sold the Beaurivage as hastily as he had bought her.

He left for town, by morning, full of bitterness at the world's conspiracy to cheat him. He felt that for a careless deck-hand to leave lemon-peel on the deck of the Beaurivage was nothing less than part of the world-wide cabal against his peace of mind.

He reached his town-house in a towering passion, all the accumulated ill-temper of the last few days bubbling in him. He flung the housedoor wide, stamped through the halls. "Nevins!" he shouted, "Nevins!"

Nothing stirred in the house. He entered room after room. Passing into his dressing-room he almost tore the hanging from its rod. A gust of air struck him from the wide-open window. Before he proceeded another step this gust, that his opening of the curtain had produced, lifted the veil from the mirror facing him. The veil swung up gently, revealed the glass, and dropped again.

Then he realized the figure of Nevins on a couch. He walked up to him. The smell of spirits met him at once.

"Poor Nevins!" he muttered.

Then he fell to further realizations.

The whole history of his three experiments unfolded itself before him. What, after them all, had he gained? What, save the knowledge of the littleness of the motives controlling those lives? This actor, this man the world thought great, whose soul he had held in usurpation, up to a little while ago, what was he? A very batch of vanities, a mountain of egoisms. Had there been, in any of the thoughts, the moods he had experienced from out the mental repertoire of that player, anything indicative of nobility, of large benevolence, of sweet and light in the finest human sense? Nothing, nothing. The ambition to imitate the obvious points of human action and conduct, to the end that one be called a character-actor; the striving for an echoed fame rightly belonging to the supreme names of history; a yearning for the stimulus of immediate acclamation—these things were not worth gaining. To have experienced them was to have caught nothing beneficial.

Orson Vane began to consider himself with contempt. Upon himself must fall the odium of what the souls he had borrowed had induced in him. The littleness he had fathomed, the depths of character to which he had sunk, all left their petty brands on him. He had penetrated the barriers of other men's minds, but what had it profited him? As a ship becalmed in foul waters takes on barnacles, so had he brought forth, from the realm of alien springs and motives he had made his own, a dreadful incrustation of painful conjectures on the supremacy of evil in the world.

It needed only a glance at the man, Nevins, to force home the destructiveness born of these incursions into other lives. That trembling, cowering thing had been, before Orson Vane's departure from the limitations of his own temperament, a decent, self-respecting fellow. While now—

Vane paced about the house in bitter unrest. In the outer hall he noticed the yellow envelopes bordering the coat-rack. He took one of them down, opened it, and smiled. "Poor Nevins!" he murmured. The next moment a lad from the Telegraph office appeared in the doorway. Vane went forward himself; there was no use disturbing Nevins.

The wire had followed him on from the Beaurivage, or rather from the man to whom he had sold her. It was from Augustus Vanlief. Its brevity was like a blow in the face.

"Am ill," it said, "must see you."

It was still possible, that very hour, to get an express to the Professor's mountain retreat. There was nothing to prevent immediate departure. Nothing—except Nevins. The man really must exercise more care about that mirror. He was safely out of all his experiments now, but the thing was dangerous none the less; if it had been his own property, he would have known how to deal with it. But it was the Professor's secret, the discovery of a lifetime. For elaborate precautions, or even for hiding the thing in some closet, there was no time. He could only rouse Nevins as energetically as possible to a sense of his previous defection from duty; gently and quite kindly he admonished him to take every care of the new mirror in the time coming. Nevins listened to him wide-eyed; his senses were still too much agog for him to realize whence this change of voice and manner had come to his master. It was merely another page in the chapter of bewilderment that piled upon him. He bowed his promise to be careful, he assented to a number of things he could not fathom, and when Vane was gone he cleared the momentary trouble in his mind by an ardent drink. The liquor brought him a most humorous notion, and one that he felt sure would relieve him of all further anxieties on the score of the new mirror. He approached the back of it, tore the curtain from its face, wheeled it to the centre of the room, and placed all the other cheval-glasses close by. Throughout this he had wit enough, or fear enough—for his memory brought him just enough picture of Orson's own handling of this mirror to inspire a certain awe of the front of the thing—never to pass in face of the mirror. When he had the mirrors grouped in close ranks, he spun about on his heels quickly, as if seized with the devout frenzy of a dervish. He fell, finally, in a daze of dizziness and liquor. Yet he had cunning enough left. He crept out of the room on his stomach, like a snake with fiery breath. He knew that the angle at which the mirrors were tilted would keep him, belly to the carpet, out of range. Then he reeled, shouting, into the corridors.

He had accomplished his desire. He no longer knew one mirror from the other.

Orson Vane, in the meanwhile, was being rushed to the mountains. It was with a new shock of shame that he saw the ravages illness was making on the fine face of Vanlief. This, too, was one of the items in the profit-and-loss column of his experiments. Yet this burden was, perhaps, a shared one.

"Ah," said Vanlief, with a quick breath of gladness, "thank God!" He knew, the instant Vane spoke, that it was Orson Vane himself who had come; he knew that there was no more doubt as to the success of his own recent headlong journeyings. They had prostrated him; but—they had won. Yet there was no knowing how far this illness might go; it was still imperative to come to final, frank conclusions with the partner in his secret.

The instant that Vane had been announced Jeannette Vanlief had left her father's side. She withdrew to the adjoining room, where only a curtain concealed her; the doors had all been taken down for the summer. She did not wish to meet Orson Vane. Over her real feelings for him had come a cloud of doubts and distastes. She had never admitted to herself, openly, that she loved him; she tried to persuade herself that his notorious vagaries had put him beyond her pale. She was determined, now, to be an unseen ear to what might pass between Orson and her father. It was not a nice thing to do, but, for all she knew, her father's very life was at stake. What dire influence might Vane not have over her father? She suspected there was some bond between them; in her father's weakened state it seemed her duty to watch over him with every devotion and alertness.

Yet, for a long time, the purport of the conversation quite eluded her.

"I have not gone the gamut of humanity," said Orson, "but I have almost, it seems to me, gone the gamut of my own courage."

Vanlief nodded. He, too, understood. Consequences! Consequences! How the consequences of this world do spoil the castles one builds in it! Castles in the air may be as pretty as you please, but they are sure to obstruct some other mortal's view of the sky.

"If I were younger," sighed Vanlief, "if I were only younger."

They did not yet, either of them, dare to be open, brutal, forthright.

"I could declare, I suppose," Vanlief went on, "that it was somewhat your own fault. You chose your victims badly. You have, I presume, been disenchanted. You found little that was beautiful, many things that were despicable. The spectacles you borrowed have all turned out smoky. Yet, consider—there are sure to be just as many rosy spectacles as dark ones in the world."

"No doubt," assented Vane, though without enthusiasm, "but there are still—the consequences. There is still the chance that I could never repay the soul I take on loan; still the horror of being left to face the rest of my days with a cuckoo in my brain. Mind, I have no reproaches, none at all. You overstated nothing. I have felt, have thought, have done as other men have felt and thought and done; their very inner secret souls have been completely in my keeping. The experiment has been a triumph. Yet it leaves me joyless."

"It has made me old," said Vanlief, simply. "Ah," he repeated, "if only I were younger!"

"The strain," he began again, "of putting an end to your last experiment has told on me. I overdid it. Such emotion, and such physical tension, is more than I should have attempted. I begin to fear I may not last very long. And in that case I think I shall have to take my secret with me. Orson, it comes to this; I am too old to perfect this marvelous thing to the point where it will be safe for humanity at large. It is still unsafe,—you will agree to that. You might wreck your own life and that of others. The chances are one in a thousand of your ever finding a human being whom God has so graciously endowed with the divine spirit as to be able to lose part of it without collapse. I have hoped and hoped, that such a thing would happen; then there would be two perfectly even, exactly tempered creatures; even if, upon that transfusion, the mirror disappeared, there would be no unhappiness as a reproach. But we have found nothing like that. You have embittered yourself; the glimpses of other souls you have had have almost stripped you of your belief in an eternal Good."

"You mean to send for the mirror?"

"It would be better, wiser. If I live, it will still be here. If I die, it must be destroyed. In any event—"

At the actual approach of this conclusion to his experiments Orson Vane felt a sense of coming loss. With all the dangers, all the loom of possible disaster, he was not yet rid of the awful fascination of this soul-snatching he had been engaged in.

"Perhaps," he argued, "my next experiment might find the one in a thousand you spoke of."

"I think you had better not try again. Tell me, what was Wantage's soul like?"

"Oh, I cannot put it into words. A little, feverish, fretful soul, shouting, all the time: I, I, I! Plotting, planning for public attention, worldly prominence. No thoughts save those of self. An active brain, all bent on the ego. A brain that deliberately chose the theatre because it seems the most spectacular avenue to eminence. A magnetism that keeps outsiders wondering whether childishness or genius lurks behind the mask. The bacillus of restlessness is in that brain; it is never idle, always planning a new pose for the body and the voice."

"Well," urged Vanlief, "think what might have been had I not put a stop to the thing. You don't realize the terrible anxiety I was in. You might have ruined the man's career. However petty we, you and I, may hold him, there are things the world expects of him; we came close to spoiling all that. I had to act, and quickly. You may fancy the difficulties of getting the mirror to Wantage. Oh, it is still all like an evil dream." He lay silent a while, then resumed: "Is the mirror in the old room?"

"Yes. With the others, in the dressing-room."

"Nevins looks out for it?"

"As always. Though he grows old, too."

Vanlief looked sharply at Orson, he suspected something behind that phrase about Nevins. Again he urged:

"Better have Nevins bring the mirror back to me."

Vane hesitated. He murmured a reply that Jeannette no longer cared to hear. The whole secret was open to her, now; she saw that the Orson Vane she loved—she exulted now in her admission of that—was still the man she thought him, that all his inexplicable divagations had been part of this awful juggling with the soul that her father had found the trick of. She realized, too, by the manner of Vane, that he had not yet given up all thought of these experiments; he wanted one more. One more; one more; it was the cry of the drunkard, the opium-eater, the victim of every form of mania.

It should never be, that one more trial. What her father had done, she could do. She glided out of the room, on the heels of her quick resolution.

The two men, in their arguments, their widening discussions, did not bring her to mind for hours. By that that time she was well on her way to town.

Her purpose was clear to her; nothing should hinder its achievement. She must destroy the mirror. There were sciences that were better killed at the outset. She did not enter deeply into those phases of the question, but she had the clear determination to prevent further mischief, further follies on the part of Vane, further chances of her father's collapse.

The mirror must be destroyed. That was plain and simple.

It took a tremendous ringing and knocking to bring Nevins to the door of Vane's house.

"I am Miss Vanlief," she said, "I want to see my father's mirror."

"Certainly, miss, certainly." He tottered before her, chuckling and chattering to himself. He was in the condition now when nothing surprised him; any rascal could have led him with a word or a hint; he was immeasurably gay at everything in the world. He reeled to the dressing-room with an elaborate air of courtesy.

"At your service, miss, there you are, miss. You walk straight on, and there you are, miss. There's the mirror, miss, plain as pudding."

She strode past him, drawing her skirt away from the horrible taint of his breath. She knew she would find the mirror at once, curtained and solitary sentinel before the doorway. She would simply break it with her parasol, stab it, viciously, from behind.

But, once past the portal, she gave a little cry.

All the mirrors were jumbled together, all looked alike, and all faced her, mysterious, glaringly.

"Nevins," she called out, "which—which is the one?"

"Ah, miss," he said, leeringly, "don't I wish I knew."

No sense of possible danger to herself, only a despair at failure, came upon Jeannette. Failure! Failure! She had meant to avert disaster, and she had accomplished—nothing, nothing at all.

She left the house almost in tears. She felt sure Vane would yield again to the temptation of these frightful experiments. She could do nothing, nothing. She had felt justified in attempting destruction of what was her father's; but she could not wantonly offer all that array of mirrors on the altar of her purpose. She stumbled along the street, suffering, full of tears. It was with a sigh of relief that she saw a hansom and hailed it. The cab had hardly turned a corner before Orson Vane, coming from another direction, let himself into his house. His conference with Vanlief had ceased at his own promise to make just one more trial of the mirror. He could not go about the business of the life he led in town without assuring himself the mirror was safe.

He found Nevins incoherent and useless. He began to consider seriously the advisability of discharging the man; still, he hated to do that to an old servant, and the man might come to his senses and his duties.

He spent some little time re-arranging the mirrors in his room. He was sure there had been no intrusion since he was there himself, and he knew Nevins well enough to know that individual's horror of facing the mirror. He himself faced the new mirror boldly enough, sure that his own image was the only one resting there. He knew the mirror easily, in spite of the robbery that the wind, as he thought, had committed.

Nevins, hiding in the corridor, watched him, in drunken amusement.

CHAPTER XIX.

The sun, glittering along the avenue, shimmering on the rustling gowns of the women and smoothing the coats of the horses, smote Orson Vane gently; the fairness of the day flooded his soul with a tide of well-being. In the air and on the town there seemed some subtle radiance, some glamour of enchantment. The smell of violets was all about him. The colors of new fashions dotted the vision like a painting by Hassam; a haze of warmth covered the town like a kiss.

His thoughts, keyed, in some strange, sweet way, to all the pleasant, happy, pretty things in life, brought him the vision of Jeannette Vanlief. How long, how far away seemed that day when she had been at his side, when her voice had enveloped him in its silver echoes!

As carriage after carriage passed him, he began to fancy Jeannette, in all her roseate beauty, driving toward him. He saw the curve of her ankle as she stepped into the carriage; he dreamed of her flower-like attitude as she leaned to the cushions.

Then the miracle happened; Jeannette, a little tired, a little pale, a little more fragile than when last he had seen her, was coming toward him. A smile, a gentle, tender, slightly sad—but yet so sweet, so sweet!—a smile was on her lips. He took her hand and held it and looked into her eyes, and the two souls in that instant kissed and became one.

"This time," he said—and as he spoke all that had happened since they had pretended, childishly, on the top of the old stage on the Avenue, seemed to slip away, to fade, to be forgotten—"it must be a real luncheon. You are fagged. So am I. You are like a breath of lilies-of-the-valley. Come!"

They took a table by an open window. The procession of the town nearly touched them, so close was it. To them both it seemed, to-day, a happy, joyous, fine procession.

"Will you tell me something?" asked the girl, presently, after they had laughed and chattered like two children for awhile.

"Anything in the world."

"Well, then—are you ever, ever going to face that dreadful mirror again?"

He smiled, as if there was nothing astonishing in her knowledge, her question.

"Do you want me not to?"

She nodded.

He put his hand across the table, on one of hers. "Jeannette," he whispered, "I promise. Why do you care? It is not possible that you care because, because—Jeannette, will you promise me something, too?"

They have excellent waiters at the Mayfair. They can be absolutely blind at times. This was such a time. The particular waiter who was serving Vane's table, took a sudden, rapt interest in the procession on the avenue.

Jeanette crumbled a macaroon with her free hand.

"You have my hand," she pouted.

"I need it," he said. "It is a very pretty hand. And very strong. I think it must have lifted all my ills from me to-day. I feel nothing but kindness toward the whole world. I could kiss—the whole world."

"Oh," said Jeannette, pulling her hand away a little, "you monster! You are worse than Nero."

"Do you think my kisses would be so awful, then? Or is it simply the piggishness of me that makes you call me a monster. That's not the right way to look at it. Think of all the dreadful people there are in the world; think how philanthropic you must make me feel if I want to kiss even those."

"Ah, but the world is full of beautiful women."

"I do not believe it," he vowed. "I do not think God had any beauty left after he fashioned—you."

He was not ashamed, not one iota of the grossness of that fable. He really felt so. Indeed, all his life he never felt otherwise than that toward Jeannette. And she took the shocking compliment quite serenely.

"You are absurd," she said, but she looked as if she loved absurdity. "Please, may I take my hand?"

"If you will be very good and promise—"

"What?"

"To give me something in exchange."

"Something in exchange?"

"Yes. The sweetest thing in the world, the best, and the dearest. You, dear, yourself. Oh! dearest, if I could tell you what I feel. Speech—what a silly thing speech is! It can only hint clumsily, futilely. If I could only tell you, for instance, how the world has suddenly taken on brightness for me since you smiled. I feel a tenderness to all nature. I believe at heart there is good in everyone, don't you? To-day I seem to see nothing but good. I could find you a lovable spot in the worst villain you might name. I suppose it is the stream of sweetness that comes from you, dear. Why can't this hour last forever. I want it to, oh, I want it to!"

"It is," she whispered, "an hour I shall always remember."

"Yes, but it must last, it can't die; it sha'n't! Jeannette, let us make this hour last us our lives! Can't we?"

"Our lives?" she whispered.

"Yes, our lives. This is only the first minute of our life. We must never part again. I seem to have been behind a cloud of doubt and distrust until this moment. I hardly realize what has happened to me. Is love so refining a thing as all this? Does it turn bitter into sweet, and make all the ups and downs of the world shine like one level, beautiful sea of tenderness? It can be nothing else, but that—my love, our—can I say our love, Jeannette?"

The sun streamed in at the window, kissing the tendrils of her hair and bringing to their copper shimmer a yet brighter blush. The day, with all its perfume, the splendor of its people, the riot of color of its gowns, the pride and pomp of its statues and its fountains, flushed the most secret rills of life.

"It is a marvel of a day," said Jeannette.

"A marvel? It is an impossible day; it is not a day at all—it is merely the hour of hours, the supreme instant, the melody so sweet that it must break or blind our hearts. You are right, dear, it is a marvelous hour. You make me repeat myself. Can we let this hour—escape, Jeannette?"

"It goes fast."

"Fast—fast as the wind. Fleet as air and fair as heaven are the instants that bring happiness to common mortals. But we must hold the hour, cage it, leash it to our lives."

"Do you think we can?"

She had used the "we!" Oh yes, and she had said it; she had said it; he sang the refrain over to himself in a swoon of bliss.

"I am sure of it," he urged. "Will you try?"

"You are so much the stronger," she mocked.

"Oh—if it depends on me—! Try? I shall succeed! I know it. Such love as mine cannot fail. If only you will let me try. That is all; just that.

"I wish you luck!" she smiled.

"You have said it," he jubilated, "you have said it!" And then, realizing that she had meant it all the time, he threatened her with a look, a shake of the head—oh, you would have said he wanted to punish her in some terrible way, some way that was filled with kisses.

"Jeannette," he whispered, "I have never heard you speak my name."

"A pretty name, too," she said. "I have wondered if I might not spoil it in my pronunciation."

"You beautiful bit of mockery, you," he said, "will you condescend to repeat a little sentence after me? You will say it far more prettily than I, but perhaps you will forgive my lack of music. I am only a man. You—ah, you are a goddess."

"For how long?" she asked. "Men marry goddesses and find them clay, don't they?"

"You are not clay, dear, you are star-dust, and flowers, and fragrance. There is not a thought in your dear head that is in tune with mere clay. But listen! You must say this after me: I—"

"I—"

"Love—"

"Love—"

"You—"

"You—"

"Jeannette—"

Her lips began to frame the consonant for her own name, but at sight of the pleading in his gaze she stilled the playfulness of her, and finished, shyly, but oh, so sweetly.

"Orson."

The dear, delightful absurdities of the hour when men and women tell each other they love, how silly, and how pathetic they must seem to the all-seeing force that flings our destinies back and forth at its will! Yet how fair, how ineffably fair, those moments are to their heroes and heroines; how vastly absurd the rest of the sad, serious world seems to such lovers, and how happy are the mortals, after all, who through fastnesses of doubt and darkness, come to the free spaces where the heart, in tenderness and grace, rules supreme over the intellect, and keeps in subjection, wisdom, ignorance and all the ills men plague their minds with!

When they left the Mayfair together their precious secret was anything but a secret. Their dream lay fair and open to the world; one must have been very blind not to see how much these two were in love with each other. They had gone over every incident of their friendship; they had stirred the embers of their earliest longings; they had touched their growing happiness at every point save where Orson's steps aside had hurt his sweetheart's memory. Those periods both avoided. All else they made subject for, oh, the tenderest, the most lovelorn conversation thinkable. It was enough, if overheard, to have sickened the whole day for any ordinary mortal.

One must, to repeat, have been very stupid not to see, when they issued upon the avenue, that they shared the secret that this world appears to have been created to keep alive. Love clothed them like a visible garment.

Luke Moncreith could never have been called blind or stupid. He saw the truth at once. The truth; it rushed over him like a salt, bitter, acrid sea. He swallowed it as a drowning man swallows what overwhelms him. One instant of terrible rage spun him as if he had been a top; he faced about and was for making, then and there, a scene with this shamelessly happy pair. But the futility of that struck him on the following second. He kept his way down the avenue, emotions surging in him; he felt that his passions were becoming visible and conspicuous; he took a turning into one of the streets leading eastward. A sign of a wineshop flashed across his dancing vision, and he clung to it as to an anchor or a poison. He found a table. He wanted nothing else, only rest, rest. The wine stood untasted on the bare wood before him. He peered, through it, into an unfathomable mystery. This chameleon, this fellow Vane—how was it possible that he had won this glorious, flower-like creature, Jeannette? This man had been, as the fancy took him, a court fool, a sporting nonentity, and a blatant mummer. And what was he now? By the looks of him, he was, to-day—and for how long, Moncreith wondered—a very essence of meekness and sweetness; butter would not think of melting in his mouth. What, in the devil's name, what was this riddle! He might have repeated that question to himself until the end of his life if the door had not opened then and let in Nevins.

Nevins ordered the strongest liquor in the place. The sideboard on Vanthuysen Square might be empty, but Nevins had still the money. As for the gloomy old Vane house, he really could not stand it any longer. He toasted himself, did Nevins, and he talked to himself.

"'An now," he murmured, thickly, "'ere's to the mirror. May I never see it again as long as I 'as breath in my body and wits in me 'ead. Which," he observed, with a fatuous grin, "aint for long. No, sir; me nerves is that a-shake I aint good for nothin' any more. And I asks you, is it any wonder? 'Ere's Mr. Vane, one day, pleasant as pie. Next day, comes in, takes a look at that dratted mirror of the Perfessor's, and takes to 'igh jinks. Yes, sir, 'igh jinks, very 'igh jinks. 'As pink tea-fights in his rooms, 'angs up pictures I wouldn't let me own father see—no, sir, not if 'e begged me on his bended knee, I wouldn't—and wears what you might call a tenor voice. Then—one day, while you says 'One for his Nob' 'e's 'imself again. An' it's always the mirror this, an' the mirror that. I must look out for it, an' it mustn't be touched, and nobody must come in. And what's the result of it all? Me nerves is gone, and me self-respect is gone, and I'm a poor miserable drunkard!"

He gulped down some of his misery.

"Join me," said a voice nearby, "in another of those things!"

Nevins turned, with a swaying motion, to note Moncreith, whose hand was pointing to the empty glass before Nevins.

"You are quite right," he went on, when the other's glass had been filled again, "Mr. Vane's conduct has been most scandalous of late. You say he has a mirror?"

All circumspection had long since passed from Nevins. He was simply an individual with a grievance. The many episodes that, in his filmy mind, seemed to center about that mirror, shifted and twisted in him to where they forced utterance. He began to talk, circuitously, wildly, rapidly, of the many things that rankled in him. He told all he knew, all he had observed. From out of the mass of inane, not pertinent ramblings, Moncreith caught a glimmer of the facts.

What a terrible power this must be that was in Orson Vane's possession! Moncreith shuddered at the thought. Why, the man might turn himself, in all but externals—and what, after all, was the husk, the shell, the body?—into the finest wit, the most lovable hero of his time; he might fare about the world wrecking now this, now that, happiness; he might win—perhaps he actually had, even now, won Jeannette Vanlief? If he had, if—perhaps there was yet time! There was need for sharp, desperate action.

He plunged out of the place and toward Vanthuysen Square. Then he remembered that he could not get in. He aroused Nevins from his brutish doze. He dragged him over the intervening space. Nevins gave him the key, and dropped into one of the hall chairs. Moncreith leaped upstairs, and entered the room where the mirror stood, white, silent, stately.

He contemplated everything for a time. He conjured up the picture he had been able to piece together from the rambling monologues of Nevins. He wondered whether to simply smash in the mirrors—he would destroy them all, to make sure—by taking a chair-leg to them, or whether he would carefully pour some acid over them.

The simpler plan appealed most to him. It was the quickest, the most thorough. He took a little wooden chair that stood by an ebon escritoire, swung it high in the air and brought it with a shattering crash upon the face of the Professor's mirror.

But there was more than a mere crash. A deadly, sickening, stifling fume arose from the space the clinking glass unbared; a flame burst out, leaped at Moncreith and seized him. The deadly white smoke flowed through the room; flame followed flame, curtains, hangings, screens went, one after the other, to feed the ravenous beast that Moncreith's blow had liberated. The room was presently a seething furnace that rattled in the cage of the walls and windows. Moncreith lay, choked with the horrid smoke, on the floor. The flames licked at him again and again; finally one took him on the tip of its tongue, twisted him about, and shriveled him to black, charred shapelessness.

The windows fell, finally, out upon the street below. The fire sneaked downward, laughing and leaping.

When the firemen came to save Orson Vane's house, they found a grinning, sodden creature in the hall.

It was Nevins. "That settles the mirror!" was all he kept repeating.

CHAPTER XX.

The Professor shivered a little when Jeannette came to him with her budget of wonderful news. She told him of her engagement. He patted her head, and blessed her and wished her happiness. Then she told him of her visit to Vane's house. It was at that he shivered.

He wondered if Vane had taken her image from that fatal glass. If he had, how, he wondered, would this experiment end? Surely it could not have happened; Jeannette was quite herself; there was no visible diminution of charm, of vitality.

When Vane arrived, presently, the Professor questioned him. The answer brought the Professor wonder, but he did not count it altogether a calamity. There could be no doubt that Orson Vane was now wearing Jeannette's sweet and beautiful soul as a halo round his own. Well, mused Vanlief, if anything should happen to Jeannette one can always—

"Oh, father!"

Jeannette burst into the room with the morning paper from town. "Orson's house is burnt to the ground. And who do you think is suspected? Luke Moncreith! They found his body. Read it!"

The Professor took the report and scanned it. There could be no doubt; the mirror, the work of his life, was gone. He could never fashion one like it. Never—Yet—He looked at the two young people at the window, whither they had turned together, each with an arm about the other.

"What a marvel of a day!" Jeannette was saying.

"The days will all be marvels for us," said Orson.

"The days, I think, must have souls, just as we have. Some days seem to have such dark, such bitter thoughts.

"Yes, I think you are right. There are days that strike one as having souls; others that seem quite soulless. Beautiful, empty shells, some of them; others, dim, yet tender, full of graciousness."

"Orson!"

"Sweetheart!"

"Do you know how wonderfully you are changed? Do you know you once talked bitterly, as one who was full of disappointments and disenchantments?"

"You have set me, dear, in a garden of enchantment from which I mean never to escape. The garden is your heart."

Something glistened in the Professor's eyes as he listened. "God, in his infinite wisdom," he said, in a reverent whisper, "gave her so much of grace; she had enough for both!"

Printed in Great Britain
by Amazon

52206545R00051